WE WHO SURVIVED

(THE FIFTH ICE AGE)

By
STERLING NOEL

ARMCHAIR FICTION
PO Box 4369, Medford, Oregon   97501-0168

*For more information about Armchair Books and products, visit our
website at…*

www.armchairfiction.com

Or email us at…

armchairfiction@yahoo.com

THE SNOW BEGAN ON A SATURDAY...

It was a cold, brooding day in September of 2203. The world's leading scientists—grimly aware of the monstrous new age of ice that would close around the Earth and bury the human race alive—had issued their warnings.

But the governments had ignored them, issued bland reassurances and berated the scientists for their alarmist cries of doom. For several years, though the snows started and stopped, the winters grew longer and the days colder.

Then one day the snow began to fall—and did not stop.

CAST OF CHARACTERS

DR. GABRIEL HARROW
Acknowledged as the foremost weather savant on the planet, but his plan for the world was a desperate one!

PROF. JACK OSBORNE
He wasn't about to try to pacify the people with inaccurate scientific drivel that would lead millions to their death!

ELAINE HARROW
She was full of knowledge and energy, yet she was the calming factor when the going got tough.

BILL WERNECKE
The double and triple checks he made of critical computations were imperative for survival.

RANCE GOODRICH
His new snow mobile design was the only thing that would get them through the perpetual winter…alive.

VICTOR SAVAGE
Missile pilots were a thing of the past in a world of endless snow storms. His new mission…snow mobile pilot!

GEORGIA LAWRENCE
Marriage restricted all her primal impulses. Unfortunately her greatest excitement was getting another woman's man!

STEVE ENGLES
His mother played him like a fiddle, but when he found a new heart throb, the war was on and he was caught in the middle!

BOOK ONE

The Storm

CHAPTER ONE

THE MANY PERSONS familiar with the statistics of the Fifth Ice Age are aware that some 100,000 persons from the North American Continent and from Europe West were able to escape from these deadly latitudes of cold, wind and snow to the narrow Equatorial belt where life on Earth remained supportable. Thus one could expect at least that many accounts of tribulation and indomitable will would, very likely, equal or surpass this report of the Savage Company (originally the Harrow Group) in their fight to survive in a world suddenly become uninhabitable.

I was unusually fortunate in being able to save all of the notebooks of Dr. Gabriel Harrow as well as my own diaries, so I am able to present a report filled with much detail.

Any report must have a beginning and I shall begin mine with a Saturday in September of 2203—the day the snow started.

CHAPTER TWO

I WAS PERMITTED to resign my Commission in the Republic of North America Air Force in 2203 because of the technicality over-age in grade. The fact that I was a Missiles Group Commander would be the real reason. There were no more Missiles Groups. Missiles pilots were as obsolete as automobiles and the missiles jockeys of the New Air Force didn't get any closer to their vehicles than an electronic control center hundreds of miles away.

So I got a job with Boren Industries in Missouri Center supervising the final assembly of Lopez Rectifiers and I wrote a long letter to Marge Couzins in Portland Complex and told her I was once and for all back on earth and available. I wrote three pages of pledges and when I went out to mail them at the post office, so that she would get my missive the next morning, it had started to snow.

I remarked on the snow, of course. Everybody did. In fact, the whole world had been remarking and complaining and predicting about the weather for several years, and particularly since the spring, which had started with twenty-seven days of drenching rain accompanied by high winds and near-freezing temperatures. There had been a respite of a few weeks, then the rain and cold had resumed and it had remained that way all summer.

By the time September had arrived there was a definitely discernible undercurrent of fear and apprehension wherever and whenever groups of people gathered. There was a feeling of impending disaster, and I believe we were all affected by it.

The Government and innumerable groups of intelligent citizens were doing their utmost to counteract this incipient panic, but they were not gaining noticeable headway. Then the sudden beginning of the mid-September snow and its accompanying cold wave of sub-zero temperatures seemed to put the lid on the pot, and the fury of doom-criers was redoubled.

Much of this pessimism, of course, was not yet in evidence on the Saturday afternoon that I walked through the early snow to the post office.

I had received an urgent summons that morning from Elaine Harrow to have dinner with her and Dr. Gabriel Harrow at their farm at Fallon, across the river in Kansas, and I walked from the post office to the Board of Trade Building, where I got an ML taxi on the roof. I started for Kansas about six o'clock, hoping that I would find a haven from the doom-talk at the safe home of my friends. That was six o'clock on September 14th, 2203. Ten minutes later I was at the Harrow's jetshield. I walked through about three inches of snow to the front door and was admitted by Elaine, dressed in Fincham arctics. Elaine was a small, dark woman in her thirties, but looked most of the time like twenty-four or twenty-five. She could wear slacks—or even Fincham arctics—with more style than a Paris opening. But the highball in her hand rattled its ice as she gestured me into the living room. A frown creased her forehead.

"Come in, Vic, hurry," she said. "Did you ever see anything like this insane weather?"

I closed the door against the swirling snow and followed her into the huge living room. She went to a sideboard and mixed me a Scotch. "Something worrying you?" I asked.

She turned to me with my drink in her hand and gave me a questioning look. "Did you hear the six o'clock news?" she demanded. "President Gamberelli's statement?"

"No."

"The President said there is nothing to fear but fear itself—that we should close our ears to the alarmists who say that we are all about to be engulfed by vast glaciers. He said there is no basis for alarm and he quoted Alex Vidal and Duncan Curran and a couple of others I never heard of. Then, near the end, he mentioned Gabe by name. He said, 'It is unfortunate that in this hour of alleged peril we have been unable to obtain the reassurance of such men as Dr. Gabriel Harrow and Professor Jack Wheeler Osborne.' Then some more tripe about how it was the duty of our great scientists to keep the public informed of the facts and reassured... I've never been so angry! What right has he got to criticize Gabe and Jack Osborne in a public broadcast?"

"Where *is* Gabe?" I asked.

"He's on his way."

"Simmer down," I said. "Why didn't Gabe and Professor Osborne give Gamberelli a statement?"

"How would I know?" she demanded. "Gabe will tell you when he comes in. But whatever the reason, it doesn't give that cheap politician the right—"

"Wait a minute," I interrupted, "we're getting to the crux of this. Does Gabe support this disaster talk?"

"No—not disaster talk. But he has a sound theory about what is happening, and he isn't going to back up a lot of wild statements by Gamberelli and the politicians. He's been with Jack Osborne and Bob Jordan for weeks now at Mt. Hood, and he wouldn't refuse to reassure the people unless he had a good reason."

"That figures. Are you sure he's coming home to dinner tonight?"

"Of course I'm sure. I just talked to him. He's in a Jupiter one-o-eight over Cheyenne, so he'll be here in less than a half-hour. But that Gamberelli!"

CHAPTER THREE

DR. GABRIEL HARROW had been my professor of Meteorology at the Academy and was acknowledged even twenty years ago to be one of the foremost weather savants in the world. Most of you must remember the wide attention he received following his discoveries in high altitude pressure phenomena, now known as the Harrow Oscillations, which subsequently won him the Barstow Award and the Nobel Prize.

In accord with the Packman Priorities of 2138, he had been required to spend seven years with private industry and had gone with Boren in Kansas City in 2198, two years after the Second Chinese War. That accounted for my connection with Boren, for Dr. Harrow and I had remained close friends since the Academy.

It was a friendship difficult to account for, beyond the fact that we were both interested in reviving the centuries old game of playing cards known as "Bridge." This is a game that was played by our forefathers with a deck of fifty-two cards, numbered from one to ten and—well, I won't bore you with our delvings into antiquity. Suffice it to say that we both found enormous pleasure in this pastime.

Elaine, who had been Gabe's research assistant at Eastern where he had done his work on the Harrow Oscillations, had also become a Bridge addict, and I believe it was this mutual interest in the game more than anything else that led to their marriage. That, of course, is an outsider's view, and I'm probably as wrong as a Chinese promise. However, it was our custom to play this game two or three nights a week whenever we were in the same areas, and so our friendship continued.

Elaine told me on this Saturday night that Bill Wernecke, chief engineer of the Boren Electronics Divisions, also was expected, so I assumed the summons had been for a Bridge game. Wernecke, like Gabe, was serving his time in private industry under the Packman Priorities. I asked Elaine when he'd be along, and she said he was doing some mathematics for Gabe and would be late.

Presently we heard Gabe Harrow's Jupiter-Ring at the jetshield. In minutes he was through the door, kissing Elaine.

Gabe was a tall, thin Grandville of a man with a head bald as a borhke ball and the most engaging voice you have ever listened to. He had as much energy as a K-11 and you seldom saw him sit still for more than a few minutes.

"Well, Vic," he exclaimed, shaking my hand, "just the man I wanted to see. Got some important questions to ask you."

"Let's have dinner first," said Elaine. "You can ask your questions while we eat. The Arabs are off at 8:00 tonight, and if we don't finish before they leave I'm going to have to clear the table and straighten out the kitchen myself."

We went to the dining room and were served an excellent repast by fat Sarah, cooked by her spouse Ali. Gabe ate the first two courses in silence and seemed completely wrapped up in his own thoughts. Elaine had attempted several times to tell him about Gamberelli, but he wouldn't listen. Her anger had cooled enough so that she wasn't very insistent. Then, with the roast fowl, Gabe turned to me and said, "Osborne and Jordan have been doing some exceptional work out at Hood. They've got an interferometer out there so sensitive they've been able to get a Doppler effect thirty billion light years out. Brother!"

"That what you've been working on at Hood?" I asked.

"No," he replied. He dropped his knife and fork and got up and walked around the table. He stopped and kissed the top of Elaine's head, then faced me. "We're on the track of something out there," he said. "Vic, this is something sensational! Another week of observations should do it. Then we'll know for sure."

"Eat your lannie-hen before it gets cold," said Elaine. "You can talk sitting down. I've seen you do it."

Gabe kissed the top of her head again and returned to his seat. He started to eat furiously, then as suddenly stopped. "We think the Solar System is just entering a great area of cosmic debris," he said. "It is our guess that we have entered the outer boundaries of this mess of dust and gas and that the concentration grows with each passing day. What can you tell me about high level dust, Vic?"

"Not much," I replied. "I took my last missile up in July and had a jaunt up to Plymouth Eighteen Platform which, as you know, is now electronically manned. I didn't notice anything unusual and I wasn't tuned in for any reports from the Platform. On the way back all of the Bissell circuits conked out so the recordings weren't of any value. However, when I got back, two of my Paxton tubes were clogged. It must have been meteor dust, as I reported at the time."

"And this happened last July?"

"July twenty-first. I was out two weeks later. Why don't you ask the Space Office? They'd know about the dust concentration if anyone would."

"They don't," he said. "I've been asking them for months and all I get is McHenry gobbledygook. The fact is, they are no longer interested in meteor concentrations and haven't been since they enfolded to their pink hearts the so-called Cable Law, dreamed up by that knucklehead Casper Cable. Casper had said the last word on the composition of space and they assume only an idiot would seek observational verification of the Law. Well, what happened before then? Any unusual dust?"

"Several clogged Paxton tubes, but I don't remember the dates. I'll check around with various pilots and see if any of them noticed anything. What period are you interested in?"

"From the first of the year up to the present. We need verification of certain specific phenomena before we can be sure where we stand, and you high level pilots are the only ones who can give it to us. But time is getting short. I can't give you longer than forty-eight hours."

"I'll start phoning first thing in the morning," I promised.

"Let me know the information by Monday midnight at Hood," he said. "I don't know that we can do anything about it, but at least we'll know the truth."

"What truth?" asked Elaine.

"Whether or not we're all going to freeze to death," replied Gabe. "Now how about some dessert?"

CHAPTER FOUR

BILL WERNECKE arrived at 10:30 A.M. in a new Caravell, and Gabe and I went out to look at it. The ground-heaters had been turned on and the snow was melted to the jetshield, but on the sides of the walk it was now about ten inches deep. It wasn't snowing very hard—just steady. The

Caravell was the traditional Ring design but powered with a single new Victarium burner mounted in the central nascelle. Wernecke fired up the burner and we took a fast five-minute hop over Missouri Center. You couldn't see a thing above 500 feet except the white snowflakes reflected in our lights.

On the way back Gabe asked him, "What do the equations show, Bill?"

"It works out to seventy-two years generally, but it depends upon which constants you use," he replied.

"We'll have to get you more figures," said Gabe. "I expected we'd be up in the hundreds."

"It doesn't work out that way," said Bill. "On the other problem, the answer is negative. The temperatures will flatten out from thirty-seven degrees above zero to eighty below from pole to pole."

Gabe shook his head, perplexed. "A swing of one hundred degrees is twice as much as I looked for. I'll have to collect more data on that, Bill."

"That's the way it adds up, right out of the Morley Computer. I tried another equation on the Tin Brain, Gabe, and I think you'll be interested in the answer. I put together all of the data on both problems, arranging it in the alpha-beta cycle, and made zeta the various constants you gave me for the cosmic cloud extent. The answers all came out within thirty days. What they amount to is this: It will take eleven months, more or less, before the leveling off period, assuming we have reached the average concentration area of the cloud. In other words, eleven months from today the temperatures will vary from a maximum of thirty-seven degrees Fahrenheit to a minimum of eighty below."

"If the rest of the data is correct," said Gabe morosely. "Let me see what further figures I can gather at Hood in the next few days. I'll call you no later than Tuesday night."

We landed back at the jetshield and went into the house for two hours of Bridge. Gabe was his usual nervous self, and his mind was less on the game than I had ever seen him.

After the last rubber (of Bridge) I asked the plain question: "What is all of this about, Gabe? What is it that is going to last seventy-two years? And when will the temperatures from pole to pole go below freezing?"

He faced me, his hands on the back of Elaine's chair.

"It's the cosmic dust cloud," he said. "What it amounts to is that we may be entering a new Ice Age. We don't know yet—we haven't completed measuring the extent of the cloud, but it would appear at this stage that the very least we can expect in extent is seventy-two years. In other words, it will take us at least that long to pass through it. But we have another week of observations at least before we can begin to be certain, however, so I would advise the cautious view at this time."

"The cautious view!" said Elaine with scorn. "We'll sit here and freeze to death while you observe!"

"You won't freeze to death this coming week. I promise you that, my pet."

"Would you mind telling me," I said, "what a cosmic dust cloud has to do with a frozen world?"

"Cause and effect," he said. "The debris brings on the ice. This was a theory first hatched some three hundred and fifty years ago and long since discarded by our more erudite scientists. It was known in the Dark Centuries as the Greenhouse Theory and it was offered to explain the four Ice Ages that the world passed through eons ago.

"The greenhouse effect is simply that our atmosphere, and principally the water vapor in it at twenty thousand feet or so, act like the roof of a greenhouse and keep in all the heat, from the sun and from infra-red radiations, so that the temperature of Earth remains relatively constant. Thus, the only way the constancy of Earth's temperature could be disturbed would be for the character of our atmospheric roof to be altered.

"What would alter it? Meteors would. If they were present in large enough concentration they would cause the water vapor in the upper atmosphere to condense and fall as rain or snow. As a matter of fact, there is observational support for this, because every year on January twelfth and thirteenth there is a tendency for exceptionally heavy precipitation, and, as every missile or rocket pilot knows, the earth passes through a heavy concentration of meteors on these days.

"Well, what we think is happening right now is that Earth has reached an area of great debris concentration consisting of meteors, meteorites, and gas, left in space by an exploded nova.

"There is much evidence that this high level condensation process has already started—that it might have begun even a hundred years ago, and that it has been increasing at a more or less steady rate ever since. I can find no indication that this precipitation will not be continuous, outside of a few hours of recess beginning Friday afternoon.

"Meanwhile, the only safe assumption is that the precipitation will continue for at least seventy-two years. As the water vapor of the upper air decreases and finally vanishes altogether, the Earth will lose its heat. We are trying to find out how cold it will get. Perhaps Bill Wernecke's first figures will prove correct—that the temperatures will vary from thirty-seven degrees above to eighty below. I hope so. In that event, we will know that existence will not be impossible. The other very hopeful indication is that we may attain this temperature area in eleven months. In that case, our problem will be only to devise ways of existing during the first period of abysmal cold and violent storms which are about to descend upon us, then to get to the warm belt of thirty-seven degree temperatures. That, of course, probably will be at the Equator, if there is no disturbance of Earth's axial balance.

"We will need a great many more observations at Hood before we can be certain of this, however."

"I'm going to Hood with you," Elaine told him. "I refuse to stay here alone and face the panic when the people find out about this."

"They won't find out," said Gabe. "Gamberelli and his Government will make certain of that."

CHAPTER FIVE

I SPENT SUNDAY and Monday on telephones around the world talking to some fifty close friends in and out of the N.A. Air Force. I moved about Missouri Center, making no more than two calls from each station. This was one of the basic dodges to avoid monitoring, and it seldom failed to work.

However, I turned up only five reports of clogged Paxton tubes and two DX-Recording Tapes (which registered intake impurities). The DX Recorders were generally obsolete by 2203, along with intake valves. Fewer than 20 missiles of the old design, with Paxton tubes, had remained in service. Of these only five had made any sorties since the first of the year. I couldn't locate the pilot of the fifth, who was reported to be up a mountainside in Japan with a native female.

I called Gabe at Hood at midnight Monday. His dynamic visage came on the scope like a breath of fresh air. "What have you got, Vic?" he asked, his eyes glittering with anticipation.

"Not much," I said. "Five clogged Paxton tubes and two DX Recordings."

"Wonderful!" he exclaimed. "Give me all the altitudes and dates and let me have a look at the recordings. I'll copy them from the scope so I can study them."

It took him twenty minutes, and then he brought Elaine on the scope and we had a three-way visit.

"I've been reading hydrogen signals," said Elaine. "We're coming to a huge cloud of it that extends thirty light years out."

"What does that mean?" I asked.

"We're measuring the area of debris," said Gabe, "but we've still got to determine the dust concentration. Everything depends upon that."

"Anything more I can do?" I asked.

"Start collecting food concentrates," said Elaine. "We're planning a large group—eighteen or twenty persons—so you'll need tons."

"Get a couple of years' supply," said Gabe. "Get them out to Fallon and we'll all meet there the end of the week. How deep is the snow there now?"

"Officially, thirty inches," I said. "Actually, nearer forty and it's beginning to drift. The wind has come up considerably in the past twenty-four hours."

"It'll come up a lot more," said Gabe. "In a month we'll have nothing but gales and hurricanes."

"My God!" I exclaimed, "shouldn't we get out?" It was purely a reflex question.

Gabe laughed. "Out where? Would you prefer the moon?"

"Not this winter," I said. "Well, all right. I'll get food."

"I've got a list of what we'll want," said Elaine. "We'll send you money—or an authorization to use our bank account, if you'd prefer."

"I've got enough money," I said. "Put your list on the copy circuit. How about reactor fuel? How are you fixed at Fallon?"

"We're okay on that, but a spare core might be useful," said Gabe.

"I forgot more arctics," said Elaine. "Get me a couple of suits, size ten—or a big eight. White."

I was looking at the list as it came through the copy slot. It did look like enough to last us the rest of our lives—all except the food.

"Let's get back to the food," I said. "Why only two years' supply?"

"More than that would be a waste," said Gabe. "If we don't figure this out before two years, there won't be any of us left to figure. In two years' time the snow will be at least a half a mile deep, and all of the lower strata for a couple of hundred feet will be solid ice due to compression. The ice won't be standing still. It'll be moving—the glacial action. We'll have to be up on the surface long before then and on our way to the warm belt—that is, if the gales and hurricanes permit us any movement."

"My God!" I exclaimed. "No alternative?"

"I don't think so. I'm still hunting. See you Saturday."

CHAPTER SIX

ON TUESDAY I obtained an indefinite leave of absence from Boren. I put in a sell-at-market order at Doble Sons for various stocks and bonds I had accumulated over the years and then went to N.A. National and cashed in my government bonds. I had 37LOOO in my hands by 1:00 P.M. and this put me 9LOOO over the government limit, so I had to do a lot of fast spending to keep out of trouble. (I suppose everyone knows about the money restrictions that followed the Second Chinese War, so I won't go into them here.)

I went first to the Cavanaugh Radical and ordered five tons of food concentrates of every flavor invented and arranged for their delivery at Fallon that afternoon by chartered Garbut. That took the pressure off my hoard of louvres by 11L000, so the rest of the day I shopped at leisure. My best buy was one of the new Kincadium Reactors, no larger than a handbag and designed to put out 23,000 Kelley units during the 20-year life of the fuel. In old-fashioned figures, this would be enough to operate a 100,000-kilowatt generator for some 50 years.

I got back to my apartment at Killingworth at 6:30 and put in a call for Marge Couzins. The scope came on prematurely and I saw Marge gesturing to a bald business tycoon type to leave the room and heard her call him Alfred. That's one of the bad features of the scope system; it can catch you with your hair down if you don't keep your circuits closed. Then Marge's smiling face came on close up, and she gave me a warm enough greeting.

"You get my letter?" I asked her.

"Yes, I got it."

"Well?"

"Well what?"

"I take it you're not interested."

"Of course I'm interested, Vic. It's just that—I can't talk right now."

"I know," I said. "The door is open and Alfred is listening."

She blushed. "Vic! What are you talking about?"

"About Alfred. I guess he's your type, Marge. Solid, dependable, a good husband who will be home every night to let you wash out his socks and cook his dinner. You're no longer the Lieut. Marge Couzins of NAAF I knew in India East a couple of years ago."

She shook her head at me, her face serious. "Don't say things like that, Vic. We haven't been together for more than a year now. You've been living your own life and there was no place in it for me. Now all of a sudden you decide to change and you expect me to come a-running."

"Can you come to Kansas tomorrow? I'll tell you all about it then."

"I have to be in Portland all this week. Would next week do?"

"Next week will be too late, Marge. You've got to come no later than Saturday."

"After sixteen months, I don't believe there is such a great hurry. Why didn't you call me last January? Did you forget that we were to have gone to the Mediterranean together for the Winter Festival?"

"Let's forget all that," I said. "You come to Fallon, Kansas tomorrow, and I'll have a padre waiting and we'll get married."

She laughed and it was like the tinkle of silver bells. "A padre," she exclaimed. "You know I don't believe in those old-fashioned ceremonies! If I am to be your wife, then we will just announce it on the DW-Three, as all civilized persons do. A marriage ceremony with a padre! Of all things!"

"All right," I said, "have it your way. But please, Marge, come to Fallon tomorrow."

"I'll try to fix things to get away Saturday," she said. "Tomorrow is out of the question."

"Fine. Saturday, then. The home of Dr. Gabriel Harrow at Fallon. He's got his own jetshield and all the taxis know it. The number is KR Forty-eight, in case you get lost. And give my love to Alfred."

"Lunger!" she exclaimed as she turned off the scope.

CHAPTER SEVEN

WEDNESDAY AND THURSDAY I stowed the food and other purchases throughout the Harrow house, with the aid of the Arabs and Sam Houston Lawrence, from the adjoining farm. By Thursday the snow had reached five feet, and the wind had increased to half a gale. I talked to Elaine and Gabe Thursday evening and they told me they were getting ready to return Friday instead of Saturday.

"I'm afraid now that everything will be shut down by Saturday," Gabe said. "I didn't anticipate the wind coming up as fast as it did, but you can't predict weather such as this. We've got a whole new set of forces to contend with. But I'll get the hang of it."

"What's the answer on the extent and concentration of the cosmic dust?" I asked him.

"It's all been worked out by Bill Wernecke and his computer. We'll be through the cloud in about one hundred and twenty-two years—not seventy-two years as he first figured. There's enough dust up there to form a dozen Earths, and when we get in the center of the cloud it will be thick enough to dim out the sun—if any sunlight could get through our storms. That will be the worst period, but it shouldn't last more than six or seven years. What will save us from complete obliteration is the speed at which this cloud is traveling, plus our own speed through it."

"So, what do we do, Gabe?"

"We sit tight, for the time being. In less than a year the storm should settle down into a definite pattern with well-defined temperature boundaries. It won't be nearly as bad as in the initial stage. There will be varying wind forces and varying precipitation in the different latitudes, and around the Equator there will form a belt of relatively mild weather that will be habitable."

"Then, for God's sake, let's head for the Equator!" I exclaimed.

"No, it'll be just as bad or worse there in the early stages as it will be here," he said. "If we went there now we'd surely perish. We've just got to sit tight here. When the time comes we'll move."

"If we can," I said.

"I'm working on something for that," he said. "I've got Rance Goodrich designing a vehicle for us. If he can't do it, nobody can."

"Okay, Gabe. I'll stop worrying."

Elaine came on the scope and I told her of my purchases and the stowage throughout the house. Both she and Gabe were quite depressed and there were few pleasantries exchanged. As soon as they disconnected, I called Marge.

"I wanted to talk to you about the weather," I said. Dr. Harrow believes this storm will last our lifetimes. We're going to have to take drastic steps to survive."

"You tell Gabe Harrow to go soak his head. I'm not going to join the weather panic."

"I don't want you to," I said. "I just want you to listen to some sense. The storm is increasing in intensity every day and by Saturday most of the world will be snowed in and immobile. So don't wait until Saturday. Come to Fallon tomorrow, and the earlier the better."

Her face got serious, and she looked at me intently out of her gray eyes. "Vic, you're not just trying to scare me?"

"No, Marge. It's merely that if we are to be together, you'll have to make up your mind that it'll be tomorrow. If you stay in Portland, you'll be safe enough. There are millions of people in the Complex who will fight the snow and fight to survive, and you will benefit by the efforts of all. Also, you're just a few miles from the Atlantic, and when all the land becomes snowbound, the sea will be the only means of travel—that is, if there is any place to which people should travel."

"Why don't you come to Portland, then?" she asked, reasonably enough.

"Our plans for Fallon have gone too far ahead," I replied. "We know that sooner or later we are going to have to leave. Gabe says it will be in about a year. We will go to the Equator, probably, but no one yet has suggested how we will get there. If this wind continues along with the snow, it's certain we're not going to get out by air. However, we're making pretty elaborate arrangements here and we'll be safe enough. Come tomorrow, Marge, please."

She thought for a moment, her eyes cast down. Then she smiled up at me. "All right," she said. "I'll be there in the morning."

"One other thing," I said. "The taxis have been grounded so I'll have to charter something fairly large for you to get from M.C. out to the farm. I'll phone in and make the arrangements. Go to the Henderson Office at the airport and they'll take care of you."

CHAPTER EIGHT

FRIDAY I was awakened some time before 4:00 A.M. in one of the Fallon guestrooms by a roar of wind that was the voice of doom itself. The whole house shook despite its steel and masonry construction. I would guess that the wind reached velocities of 150 miles per hour in gusts, and it blew at least a steady 100 M.P.H.

I got dressed and went to the kitchen, where I found Ali and Sarah sitting, huddled in worried consultation. I reassured them as best I could and sat at their table and had coffee with them. I turned on the VM receiver and found the air filled with disaster.

The hurricane winds had swept the oceans over all of the low coastal lands along the Atlantic and the Western Gulf of Mexico and had inundated at least a score of cities. York Area 1 was under five feet of water and it was feared that at least 200,000 persons had lost their lives. Most of Boston Complex was flooded and the dead there were expected to reach at least 50,000. All of the low areas of Long Island were under water, with nearly 100,000 missing and believed lost. The Jersey Complex was likewise hard hit, with another

100,000 missing, and half of Delaware Complex (the old city of Philadelphia) was wiped out, with at least 100,000 dead. The destruction went all the way down the coast to Florida, although in the far South the damage was less and the winds of lower velocity.

As the reports of the disaster mounted the feeling of panic grew. The voices on the VM reflected it so that very soon one felt himself to be in a madhouse. Ali and Sarah both were moaning and crying; then they jumped up from their seats and began to rush about aimlessly, screaming out their fear. I restrained my own impulse to join their demonstration and finally collected my wits sufficiently to turn off the VM. I calmed them somewhat after half an hour and convinced them, partially at least, that they were in no danger at Fallon.

At 5:30 A.M. I went into the library and called Mt. Hood. I got a sleepy, short-tempered Gabe Harrow on the scope. It was 2:30 A.M. out there, and he told me morosely that he'd been in bed little more than an hour.

I told him of the hurricane winds and the disasters on the Atlantic and Gulf coast—that there would probably be more than a million dead and that a major panic apparently had set in, judging from the VM.

"Don't let it upset you," he said. "The wind will last only a few hours, so it'll be forgotten soon enough. I knew about the wind. It's due out here in an hour or so, but its force should be greatly reduced by the mountains."

"How about the flooding?" I asked him.

"It's some sort of unique disturbance that started around Earth from East to West at noon yesterday. Our first reports came from Central Asia and we think it originated in the vicinity of the China coast. Now go back to bed, Vic, and let me get some sleep."

He clicked off the connection and I went back up to the guestroom. My mind was whirling like a turbine. I sat down at a desk and began to make drawings of various installations we would need if we were to exist under several hundred feet of snow.

My first thought was of ventilation, if our oxygen generators should conk out. Every home in 2203 still had its own oxygen generator, a hangover from the air contamination of the insane Fourth World War, when men had pretty nearly succeeded in exterminating each other and making the Earth uninhabitable with radioactivity.

However, the use of the generators had greatly declined in the past 25 years as the air cleared. I stopped my drawing long enough to go to the reactor room and check on the Harrow farm generator. I gave it a whirl to check on the output, then went back to my room satisfied.

The ventilator I designed was a metal tube that was to be pushed up through the snow. The length could be increased by the addition of sections of tubing, and two suction fans at the bottom would draw in the air. The main feature, actually an afterthought, was a group of instruments mounted at the upper opening for reporting the weather.

After those drawings were completed, I spent a lot of time speculating upon what manner of vehicle Rance Goodrich would design for carrying us over the snow. I began to make drawings of so-called snowmobiles, which were used back in the Dark Centuries to travel in the Arctic and Antarctic, before man had discovered the simplicities of fusion reactors and the easy way to fly. The vehicles I was drawing were, actually, variations of the ancient automobile, the chief differences being tremendous wheels of inflated rubber that would support the machine and its occupants on snow.

At 8:15 I got Bill Wernecke on the scope and put my ventilation project in his lap. The Werneckes had just finished breakfast, and I could hear Martha and the kids in the background with voices raised. I showed Bill the drawings over the scope and he praised my design and said that in his opinion it would work like a mallow.

"Save 'em," he said. "We'll see you later today. I talked to Gabe yesterday and he insists that we all come out to Fallon immediately."

"Wind do any damage at Berle Park?" I asked.

"Not to us. We heard it, though. Woke us up at three A.M. It seems to be dying down now."

"I talked to Gabe about it," I said. "It's some sort of freak disturbance."

"Probably the sun will be out this afternoon," he said. "Wouldn't be a bit surprised if this was the end of the storm—a sort of last gasp."

"A hundred to one says you won't see the sun during your lifetime," I said.

"I'll take that. One louvre's worth, and I'll collect it tonight. Keep your chin up, Colonel Savage."

He went off the scope and I went back to my designing. At ten o'clock the wind had subsided completely. I had been aware, over my concentration, that there had been a change—that something external was very different. Suddenly I realized it was the absence of wind-howl. I looked out the window (the snow had drifted up to the second-story sill) and it seemed that the snowfall had thinned out considerably. I went down to the living room and turned on the VM and the VK receivers.

Luke Hobson, Secretary for Internal Affairs, was on the VK, his fat, smiling face and his unctuous voice oozing optimism. "...that the storm is nearing its end," he said. "You will see that our predictions have been right, that these prophecies of an Ice Age and a frozen world are just so much latakia. I can assure you that it will stop snowing within hours and—"

I cut off the VK and tuned up the VM. There was a plump lady with shiny, blonde hair mixing something in a bowl and talking about it in a low, sexy voice. Life went on as usual. I cut off the VM.

At 10:41 the Garbut I had ordered from the Henderson Office set down at the jetshield and Marge Couzins was in my arms and giving me one of those kisses I once thought I couldn't live without—and apparently was ready so to think again. Marge is a tall girl, only seven inches shorter than I am, and ordinarily her heels make up for some of that difference. Today she was dressed in Fincham arctics with fur snow boots, so she was back down to her real height. She took my arm and we walked up the heated path to the house.

"You're a hell of a weather prophet," she said. "Everybody from Luke Hobson on down to the air steward says the storm is over—that there'll be no more snow after today."

"All right," I said. "You win. The storm is over. Gabe is a crackpot. How about we get married?"

"You mean a silly ceremony with a priest? I should say not!"

"Well—what do we do then? I've never been through this before."

"Neither have I. But we get three witnesses. We turn on the DW-three—there is a DW-three here, isn't there? Then you say, 'Be my wife, Marjorie Couzins.' I reply, 'I will be your wife, Victor Savage.' Then we face the screen while our picture is taken and we give our addresses and Waverly Numbers. That's all there is to it."

"I like the old fashioned way better," I said. "We would go to a temple or the priest comes here. He would read out of the ancient prayer book, then we would premise to love, honor, and obey each other and I would put a gold ring on your finger. Then we would kiss and would be married. We would get an engraved certificate that we could frame over our bed—a sort of license to make love. That's real romance!"

"Phooey," said Marge. But she gave me another one of those kisses and I didn't care much how we got married, so long as we did.

CHAPTER NINE

ON FRIDAY, September 20th, the sun came out for two hours and set in a blaze of orange and dusty red over the Missouri plains. It was the first time any of us had seen the sun for some five months, and we stood on the porch of the Harrow farm at Fallon and watched it sink to rest. There was a large gathering of us at that memorable sundown. There were Elaine and Gabe Harrow, who had flown in from Mt. Hood, bringing with them Professor Osborne and Bob and Libby Jordan. Steve Engles and his mother Cora came from York Area Two, Rance Goodrich from Jersey Complex, Florence Donner from Colorado Center, and Dr. Rufus Howard and Bill and Martha Wernecke and their two children, Alice and George, from Missouri Center. There were Marge and myself, of course, and the two Lawrence boys, Fred and Sam Houston from the next farm.

Gabe Harrow, Bob Jordan and Jack Osborne brought with them further disquieting news that seemed oddly improbable with the sun shining and the temperature rising to the 30's. They said that the abatement of the snow and the sunshine were very temporary—that the earth had been passing through a rift, or hiatus in the cosmic cloud, and that they had been able to measure its extent three days before and could predict that at 2:13 the next morning the snow and wind would begin again with redoubled violence.

Later in the evening Gabe, Osborne, Jordan, Engles, who was a former Navy commander and reactor engineer, Wernecke and I gathered in the library for the first meeting of the directors of the Harrow Group. Gabe presided, since it was his idea and his house, and he briefly outlined the agenda.

"Our problem now is simply ways and means of survival," he said.

"Vic Savage has filled this house with enough food concentrates to last us a couple of years, so food will not be the problem. Also, he had the foresight to obtain one of the new Kincadium reactors and additional fuel for our present Fornium reactor, so our problem will not fall into the areas of heat, light, and power.

"What we face are two immediate problems, mainly. There was a third—that of ventilation in the event our oxygen generator failed, but Colonel Savage has already solved it for us with his design of a vent tube that will reach to the surface of the snow when it covers us over. What remain are a safe passageway from the house to the East Barn, where all of our vital materials and our workshop and tools will be, and secondly the shoring up of our house and the barn so that they will not cave in on us with the weight of the snow.

"Bill Wernecke is applying his engineering skill to both of these situations, and I have no doubt they will be solved while we are still mobile.

"There is one more vital aspect of our condition, our escape from this place. Some time within the next twelve months the violence of the storm will subside and the precipitation will form into a more or less regular pattern for areas. Our expectation is that the heaviest precipitation will concentrate around the polar regions and that as we approach the Equator it will lessen and warmer weather will be found. In the polar regions we think a minimum of eighty degrees below zero Fahrenheit will prevail.

"At our latitude we expect the minimum temperature to hover around zero or ten below, Fahrenheit. What we expect and hope for is that at the Equator, when the storm levels off, we may find temperatures as high as plus forty degrees Fahrenheit. If we are right about that, only rain will be found at sea level in the Equatorial belt. The higher altitudes, of course, will be correspondingly colder.

"I am taking a tremendous gamble with all of our lives by installing us at Fallon, which is about one thousand miles from the sea as the Rings fly. I tell you all now, if you do not have faith in the plan I shall present, then by all means install yourselves closer to the Atlantic, your only highway South when the time comes to move. But in the meantime I think that the dangers of living near the sea are far greater than those we will encounter inland. I believe that the oceans will overrun a great deal of the Coastal lands and that destruction and loss of life will be uncountable.

"It was with this in view that I chose Fallon. We are in the center of the continent and safe from the waters of the oceans and the Gulf. We are in the flattest part of the continent, where the winds may pass freely without the tremendous pressure build-ups and resulting wild gusts found near the mountains. Also, we are surrounded on three sides by mountain ranges, which should reduce the wind force somewhat at low altitudes.

"It is also possible and quite likely that the winds in this area may reduce the snow buildup by many hundreds of feet, piling up the highest drifts in the mountainous terrain. So it is my plan to try to ride out the worst of it here, then try to get out of our own trap and get to the ocean when the time comes.

"Flying will be out of the question. The time to move will come years before the high winds subside. We can expect the hurricane winds to last some fourteen years. We will have to travel on top of the snow, and with that in view I have ordered constructed, according to the design of Rance Goodrich, a snow vehicle that should support us all in safety, if not comfort. The parts of this machine should arrive at Fallon by chartered Ring Express some time before midnight. We will have at least two hours to store the parts of our precious machine before the storm resumes.

"I was much interested to learn, upon my return home, that Colonel Savage had been working on designs of a similar machine. Here is proof that our minds are in accord and that our thinking is alike.

"Our first decision, then, should be on the question of whether we follow the Fallon plan, as outlined, or split up to seek our individual safety."

Steve Engles got to his feet and faced Gabe. Steve was several inches taller than I, but twenty pounds lighter. He had been an outstanding athlete at the Academy and I had got to know him well there, though he was two years ahead of me. He had often been a fourth at our Bridge soirees and was a powerful, aggressive contestant. He was, to my mind, a doubtful choice for a group such as ours, however, for he had an uncertain temper and no sense of humor.

"I want to know something else before we get down to voting on anything," he said. "I want to know who's number one man here?"

Gabe looked embarrassed. He didn't want to name himself, although he was the logical choice since he had assumed the leadership and responsibility from the beginning. I got up and faced Steve.

"Gabe Harrow is the boss," I said. "There are six of us on this board of directors, and in the event of a tie vote on any question his is the vote that counts, all alone… I'm not laying down any rules, Steve. I'm just making a motion. Let's vote on it."

Gabe called for the vote and the ayes were loud and clear. There was one no and it came from Steve, who had remained on his feet. I got up again. "You want to say anything about our decision?" I asked him.

"Yes, I have an opinion to express," he said.

"We'll listen to Steve," said Gabe. I sat down.

"I'll take only a moment," Steve replied calmly. "I don't know whether I want to entrust my mother's life and my own to other persons if I am not going to have any greater say in the decisions, and if she is going to have none. I don't mean to say that I have no confidence in Dr. Harrow and the rest of you, but too often in crises such as we will face, the majority opinion will result from fear and panic. Who of this group, with the possible exception of Vic Savage and, of course, myself, has been faced with the responsibility of the lives of others in a fight for survival? If Dr. Harrow's black picture of the future is correct, then we would encounter here in Fallon a grim fight indeed.

"Personally I would prefer high ground nearer the sea and close to a modern city where there would be available to us the manpower and the machines that would give us a more equal chance. It is my judgment that my mother and I should leave here and go to Richmond Complex. The California terrain of mountains adjacent to the sea is much more practicable for the conditions that Dr. Harrow foresees. I invite any or all of you to join my mother and myself."

He sat down. There was heavy silence for a couple of minutes. Here was the first doubt cast upon the Fallon Plan and the first real challenge of Gabe's judgment. I know that I had a momentary impulse to swing over to Steve's side and announce that I would go West with him. I am certain that others felt the same way, to greater or lesser degrees. What's more, he had confidence, and in the state all of us were in then, confidence counted for a great deal.

Gabe said, "I would strongly advise against it, Steve. The winds, which will be generally from West to East, will generate wild velocities in their sweep across the Pacific and they will hit the West Coast with full force. I believe you would do much better on the Atlantic Coast if you can find high enough ground, or even on the Gulf of Mexico, flat as it is down there. Some fifty miles inland might be safe enough. You and your mother have my most sincere best wishes."

Jack Osborne said, "I don't know you, Mr. Engles, but I've heard Gabe speak of you and I know he has great respect for your abilities in the field of fusion and reactors. I want to add my own small warning about the West Coast. The snows will be deeper there and the wind velocities higher than in any other section of the continent. In addition, we expect the Pacific to freeze over first. Now this may take several years—or it may occur within a year. However, I do not believe that the Pacific will be a dependable highway South."

Steve Engles said, "Well, in that case, my mother and I may revise our plans and go back east. I should like to remain for the rest of the meeting, if I may."

"By all means," said Gabe. He turned to me and said, "Vic, will you put a motion on the general question of acceptance of the Fallon Plan?"

I framed the motion, rather clumsily I thought, and all of us voted aye. Steve remained silent. Then at Gabe's request I put a second motion on the question of whether we should follow Gabe's proposal to seek to escape South by surface transportation when the time came. I realized, of course, as Gabe must have, that the proposal was at this junction a wildly optimistic notion and that first we must devise means of living through the violence immediately ahead. But anything optimistic was a sound idea on this Friday.

Both Bob Jordan and Bill Wernecke spoke on the problems of surface movement under the conditions we anticipated, then Gabe called in Rance Goodrich to explain the design of his machine, which had been dubbed a "snowmobile" after the custom of the Twentieth Century.

CHAPTER TEN

RANCE GOODRICH, ten years younger than I, was one of the most brilliant industrial designers of the Dynamics Radical and had achieved world-wide acclaim at 25 for his conception of automatic electronic control of the Plymouth Platforms. All of the current Platform installations were of his own creation, as well as the magnetic field modifiers that kept them in orbit.

"The main feature of this machine," he said, "is the wheels, which are essentially oversized inflated rubber tires, much the same kind used for this purpose in the Arctic before the age of flight. It is obvious to all of us that any airborne vehicle is more efficient for any transportation purpose than a surface vehicle, but I am assured by Dr. Harrow and others that flight will be impossible for many years because of the high winds.

"These wheels of ours, which we constructed at Dynamic, are my particular pride, for they are individually self powered with Utley Progravity Gyros, deriving their basic energy from small fusion reactors within the hubs. They will turn under any possible conditions of terrain we may encounter. The rest of the vehicle is more or less standard, with a permanium and Lomax alloy cabin large enough for twenty or so, and Lomax alloy frame and fittings.

"It is my understanding that we will not assemble our vehicle until we are ready to use it, so you will not be able to examine this obsolete marvel at present. But I hope that, when you do finally see it, you will restrain your laughter. It may save our lives."

Rance's dissertation ended the discussion, and a vote was taken immediately on whether or not we would seek to use his machine. Again the ayes were unanimous, with the exception of Steve Engles. Gabe then called for adjournment until Saturday evening.

I returned to the living room just behind Steve. He asked Florence Donner, a striking green-eyed redhead who had been Elaine Harrow's roommate at Oriental, if she had seen his mother.

"Cora's above," said Florence. "Said she had a headache."

He addressed Dr. Rufe Howard, who had been playing parch with Florence. "Do you mind coming up and having a look at her?" he said.

"Cora's healthier than you are," said Rufe. "All's the matter with her is too much imagination."

Steve clenched his fists and stood with his legs apart, glaring at Dr. Howard. "You don't know a damn thing about my mother," he said angrily.

Rufe looked up startled, then smiled. "I've known Cora longer than you have," he said quietly. "She's always had headaches—and heart palpitations—when situations were not to her liking. However, I'll go up and see her if you insist."

"Never mind!" said Steve, turning abruptly and heading for the stairway in the hall.

"Whew!" exclaimed Florence. "What a temper he's got!"

"He won't be with us, so we don't have to worry about that," I said.

"I don't think we will miss them," said Rufe Howard. "There's a classic example of the Oedipus complex, modified—or probably multiplied—by the Gerber Therapy."

"What do you suppose is going on?" asked Florence, pointing her thumb upward.

"Steve is comforting his mother," said Rufe. "He is telling her how much he loves her and how he will protect her from the bad world."

"I wish I could get a big man like him to tell me that," said Florence.

"You can," said Rufe. "Just raise a big son and give him the Gerber Series."

CHAPTER ELEVEN

AT 11:05 that night (Friday, September 20) a Garbut Transport settled softly at the jetshield at Harrow farm and we went out to help unload the snowmobile. Rance

Goodrich assumed command of the operation, since it was "his" machine, and no one objected. The rest of us—Gabe, Jack Osborne, Bob Jordan, and the two Lawrences, Fred and Sam Houston, acted as the work gang under his direction. Libby Jordan, Florence and Marge were the kibitzers (a Bridge term which means one who comments on the play of the Bridge hands) and I was elated to see that these three had so quickly accepted each other and apparently were becoming friends.

We got the Garbut unloaded in less than half an hour, with the aid of Corning jacks and a Localus carrier that, fortunately, was part of the ample equipment of the Harrow farm. We stowed the boxed parts of the snowmobile in the East Barn, which was closest to the jetshield. We had to melt a path to the barn with a Corry converter, but that took only a few minutes.

"Bill Wernecke will start reinforcement of the East Barn roof in a few days," Gabe told me. "I have all of the material he will need to reinforce the barn and the house. The West Barn is stacked to the rafters with Lomax alloy beams and siding. Before the Chinese War, I was going to build my own Ionoscope Tower and observation station. Now they're against the law... I sometimes wonder, Vic, whether Gamberelli was a wise choice for President."

"I guess it won't make much difference in a few months," I said.

"No, it won't...Is this girl you've brought the one you told Elaine and me about a couple of years ago?"

"Yes. I dropped her for a time but I couldn't forget her."

"You planning to marry her?"

"Of course."

"She looks like a good choice to me, Vic. Elaine told me she likes her very much. You've complied with the trial period regulations, I trust?"

"Oh yes. We've lived together the requisite number of days—in fact, twice the requisite. I've got the certificates somewhere."

"You'd better have them here if you're going to make it legal."

"I'm sure they're in my bag… Gabe, what do you honestly think our chances are? I know the reasons for a lot of this—the elaborate plans, the snowmobile, the board of directors. We just can't quit. It isn't in you and it isn't in any of this group you've gathered here. But—what's the answer?"

He looked at me long and hard in the dim work light that came through the open barn door. He shook his head, then, and said, "I wish the hell I knew, Vic."

CHAPTER TWELVE

RUFE HOWARD met us at the jetshield and told us that Steve Engles had sent word to hold the Garbut Transport until he and his mother could get aboard. I found the pilot and asked him if he would take mother and son to some destination on the East Coast.

"The ship belongs to Dr. Harrow until midnight," he replied. "I'll take 'em anywhere this side of the United Arab Republic."

I went back in the house and found Bill Wernecke spread out with his papers on the living room floor, working on the drawings for the reinforcement of barn and house. I asked him if he had seen Steve Engles.

"He was down here a moment ago," he said, "but I think he went back upstairs."

I went up to the second floor and along the hall that opened to the guestrooms. I heard voices coming from one and knocked on the door. Steve told me to enter.

Cora Engles was lying on the bed, a blanket drawn up under her chin. She was fluttering her eyelids in a most peculiar and difficult way.

"Oh, my heart!" she exclaimed. "I just know I am going to have another attack!"

"I'll get Dr. Howard right away," said Steve, great concern in his voice.

"Don't, please don't," said Cora, gasping between the words.

"But you must have a doctor!" said Steve.

"Not Dr. Howard," she said then, her voice suddenly firm and no-nonsense. "Get me my medicine." Then she became the fading lily. "I don't trust that Rufe Howard, Stevie."

He got her medicine, a large bottle of purple pills, then filled a glass with water in the bathroom and held her head up gently in his arm while she took a pill and a sip. He eased her back on the pillow and stood looking at her sadly.

Cora was what you would call a handsome woman, at first glance. That was the overall impression, but, as you examined her feature by feature, you were inclined to change your mind. Her mouth was too thin, her eyes were small and sharp when you looked at them closely under the makeup, and her nose was much too small for the wide cheekbones and the broad forehead. But she had kept her figure, her feet were always neat, and her legs, which she showed often, were pleasantly curved. Steve finally turned to me and opened his palms in a gesture of helplessness.

"The Garbut will take you and your mother anywhere," I said.

Cora fluttered her eyelids, then opened her eyes and looked at me for the first time. "Hello, Colonel Savage," she said. "Please excuse me for being so deathly ill. I didn't know you were in the room."

"I'm afraid my mother can't travel tonight," Steve said. "We'll have to charter a Ring in the morning."

"The morning may be too late," I said. "You heard what Gabe predicts. Of course, if the wind doesn't come up suddenly—"

"We'll just have to take that chance," he said. "You can see how ill she is."

"Don't bother about me, son," she said. "Take the transport yourself and leave me here. I'm no good to you any more."

He knelt by the bed and put his arms around her. "Don't talk that way, mother!"

I went back downstairs.

CHAPTER THIRTEEN

THERE WAS LITTLE SLEEP for any of us that Friday night. It was the first night that the members of the Harrow Group (with the exception of the Lawrences) spent together and it was a night charged with much feeling of many different hues and intensities. I think that all of us were vitally interested in what would happen at 2:13 A.M., according to Dr. Harrow's prediction. If the snow and the winds did not resume, then we would know, or suspect, that these hypotheses were in error, or at least that the observations were not accurate.

A buffet dinner was served at 7:30, with all fresh food, for the Harrows maintained a freezing unit in their basement cold-room that held a ton of meats and vegetables. Steve came from upstairs and fixed a plate for his mother and himself. He was greeted pleasantly enough, even by Dr. Howard, and he talked to everyone with relaxed charm. But when he had carried his plates up above, there was a general discussion of him and his mother. Florence Donner and Martha Wernecke, Bill's wife, put the question almost simultaneously to different knots: "Is Cora being sick just because she wants to stay with the Harrow Group?"

I think that we all agreed this was the case, and that no matter what we thought of Steve and his mother, we were going to have to put up with them, unless Gabe's prediction for 2:13 A.M. went sour.

"They won't be any burden on us, so we shouldn't regard this eventuality with such distaste," said Rufe Howard. "Actually, Steve is a competent and trustworthy member of society and Cora is just as able and efficient as any woman I've ever known, so long as she doesn't feel she has to have the vapors to get her own way."

After dinner the group disposed of itself about the farmhouse, some to read, some to talk, some to look and listen to VM or VK or the short wave programs from Europe East, but all of us to wait. Bob and Libby Jordan, Marge, Elaine and I gathered around the old-fashioned fireplace in the living room where logs were burning. We talked personalities—mostly Steve and Cora—for half an hour. Then Elaine asked, "When are you and Marge going to make it legal? Gabe tells me you've got your trial period certificate."

"We can do that any time," said Marge.

"There's a DW-three in the library if you want to do it now," said Elaine. "How about it, Vic?"

"It's up to Marge," I said.

Marge gave me an odd look, then shrugged.

Libby Jordan turned on me angrily, "If you were my fiancé, I'd drown you in the river! What's the matter with you, Vic?"

"Matter with me!" I exclaimed. "Nothing. What am I supposed to be doing that I'm not?"

"You're supposed to act just a little bit like a guy in love," said Libby. "That's what!"

I got up. I said, "All right, Marge. You've stalled long enough. We get married right away."

She sat in her chair and shook her head. "Not yet," she said.

"Yes, now," I said. "Come on." I took her by the arm and pulled her to her feet. "Now."

"No," she said. "I—well, no."

Libby said, "Listen, you ape, tell her you love her. For God's sake, haven't you any sense at all?"

Then it dawned on me—not until then. These women! They had to be told that you loved them!

I took Marge in my arms and I told her. I kissed her a couple of times and I told her some more. Finally she sighed deeply and she said yes, we could go in now and stand before the DW-three.

Marge and I walked into the library arm in arm and Libby and Elaine went to rouse the rest of the house and get them all there as witnesses. There was a lot of noise and confusion about it and finally all were assembled, even Steve and Cora, who actually looked sick by this time, and the two Arabs.

Marge and I went through the prescribed formula, and in less than two minutes we were man and wife. The men kissed Marge and the women kissed me and then we adjourned to the living room where champagne and cakes were brought out. Marge practically glowed with happiness, and I couldn't get rid of the silly grin on my face. I didn't know why I felt the way I did. I guess I really loved her. I guess I began to realize it for the first time. Then I suddenly knew, as I thought about this, that I had no more doubts—that Marge was the girl for me once and for always...I was awfully late to become aware of these feelings and this knowledge, I concede.

The party lasted until five minutes after two. Cora had gone back up to bed, but Steve remained with us. All the rest were gathered in the big living room and it was a gala affair, with music coming from the amplifiers and the wine flowing freely. Our spirits were all up and there were laughter and happy voices all about us. Marge and I stood close together in a corner, drinking our champagne out of the same glass and telling each other many small intimate confidences.

Then at 2:05 A.M. Bob Jordan announced the time. Suddenly there was a pall over the room.

CHAPTER FOURTEEN

THE GROUP WENT OUT on the porch. The temperature had nose-dived twenty degrees since midnight and was down to 18 above zero. Gabe Harrow stood with a chronometer in his hand and called off the minutes.

"Two-eight," he announced. "Temperature eighteen, wind about five knots from the West."

Marge was shivering and I put my arm around her. "I'd better get my jacket," she said.

"I'll get it for you."

"It's in the hall closet—it's black and has a beaver hood."

I went inside and found the jacket, then hurried out.

Gabe said, "Two-eleven, temperature steady at 18. Wind freshening. About eight or nine knots, I would judge."

"Thanks, darling," said Marge as I helped her into the jacket. I kissed her and she clung to me closely.

"Two-twelve," said Gabe. "Temperature seventeen. Wind at thirty knots at least... My God it's coming up fast!"

"The next announcement is it," said Elaine.

We all waited without sound or movement. Marge dug her nails into my arm and I could feel her body quivering.

"Two-thirteen," called Gabe. "No sign of snow. Temperature at sixteen. Wind now blowing half a gale."

"No snow!" exclaimed Jack Osborne.

There was general movement in the crowd. Alice Wernecke said in a high voice, "Stop it, Tony!"

Suddenly several voices called out, "There it is! Snow!"

"Two thirteen and a half," said Gabe loudly. "Well, Jack, we were thirty seconds off…must have been the wind."

CHAPTER FIFTEEN

THE WIND and the snow increased steadily for the next two hours, and by 4:15 A.M. it was blowing a full gale and the snow was so thick visibility was down to a few feet. The temperature had sunk to four above zero but Marge and I, snug in our first-floor master bedroom which had been turned over to us for our wedding night by the Harrows, lay in each other's arms and talked the night through without a care on our minds.

It was the most delightful night I had ever spent, and the joy of it and the nights immediately to follow was so pervading that it took both of us several days before we could be aware of the bleak, forbidding world of storm and violence around us. I would say that it was not until the following Tuesday morning that Marge and I became conscious of the depressed spirits of the Harrow group and took the first good look about us since Saturday night at the external world, which was slowly being wrapped in death.

On Tuesday morning the snow measured eleven feet officially and had drifted well over the second story windows on three sides of the farmhouse. Two Cory heat converters had been kept working at the front of the house, so the snow was clear there in a wide path that extended to the two barns and the jetshield. Both Marge and I joined the workers at the West Barn. We helped them to move the Lomax alloy beams to the East Barn and the house, where the interior reinforcements already had begun under the direction of Bill Wernecke.

We were welcomed to this group by Jack Osborne, Rance Goodrich and Steve Engles. Rance and Jack were untangling the beams from the pile that reached to the barn roof and

Steve was one of the carriers. (Lomax alloy, as all of you must remember, was about a third the weight of magnesium with a tensile strength far above that of old-fashioned steel.) Rance and Jack made the usual remarks about bride and bridegroom, but there was very little humor in them. Steve, who had been looking on silently, apologized for both.

"I think this storm has gotten on our nerves considerably and it is almost impossible to be light," he said. "I know that I wanted to say something, too, but I was afraid it wouldn't come off."

Marge said, "Let's just forget it. Sure, we've been doing what most of the world does all the time. We've been making love. Give me one of those beams and I'll see if I can fight my way back to the house."

Steve handed her an eight-foot beam and she tucked it under her arm and started out. I said, "I'm glad you decided to stay with us, Steve. We can use your knowledge of reactors."

He picked up several fifteen-foot beams and started for the door. "Thanks," he said. "But I haven't changed any of my views. I think Kansas is a lousy idea."

Jack Osborne climbed down from the pile and lit a cigarette. "We're going to have trouble with that monkey," he said. "He'll never take orders from Gabe when the going gets rough."

"I'll handle him when it's necessary," I said. "Meanwhile we can use his brain, Jack. Don't forget he's the only reactor expert we've got. If we start stumbling over personalities this early, we'll all murder each other before we can get out of here."

He puffed on his cigarette in silence for a moment. Then he smiled at me and whacked me on the back. "You've got some sense, Colonel," he said. "I'll remember that when I start getting moody again."

We worked continuously Tuesday at our various critical jobs and there was very little time for meals or conversation and none for recreation. The howling wind and the almost solid sheets of snow were frightening phenomena and so we battled with every ounce of our energy to build for ourselves a haven that would be safe.

The reinforcement work for house and barn shaped up very quickly and by Friday, September 27th, the work on the barn was completed and half of the house had been shored up. Bill Wernecke showed us with his drawings and stress figures that our abode would support thousands of tons of weight when the work was completed, and I know that we all felt new confidence.

By September 27th the official reports from the broadcasts placed the depth of snow at fifteen feet four inches and the wind velocity at 80 miles per hour. The temperature varied between 17 and 18 degrees below zero at 2:00 A.M. and four or five below at 2:00 P.M.

Florence Donner was appointed official broadcast monitor by Gabe and a complete set of receivers was installed in a small den off the library, which became the communications room. On the previous Tuesday she had begun typing up brief summations of the daily reports, and these were placed on a notice board in the dining room.

It was on this Friday that all air service was officially abandoned. No Rings had been able to fly since shortly after the resumption of the storm on Saturday morning and there had been a terrible loss of life during those first few hours of high winds when the thousands of Rings in the air at the time were blown to Earth. However, missiles could still operate with relative safety and efficiency, since they are only little affected by wind. The difficulty there was that passenger missiles had been abandoned years before with the development of the Spencer principle and the perfection of the Gar Ring, which operated at one-fifth the cost of the missile and at very nearly the same speed. (The Bates Rings actually were faster than missiles but were considered unsafe at speeds over 1,800 miles per hour.) Now in 2203 there were no passenger missiles in service and the few still operable in the Air Force could carry one or two persons. The great air age of the Twenty-second and Twenty-third centuries had come to an abrupt end.

York Area One had been completely wiped out as an area of human habitation. Only parts of Long Island Complex remained habitable. Half of Boston Complex had been destroyed. Most of the smaller Centers, Cities and Towns along the Atlantic Coast from Portland Complex to Charleston Complex had ceased to exist. Delaware Complex had lost half of its habitations and Baltimore Complex was under ten feet of water and ice. Most of Jersey Complex and Jersey Center had, miraculously, escaped destruction, and most of York Area Two was intact.

The estimates of the dead on the Atlantic Coast alone ran anywhere from eight to twelve million persons.

Inland from the Atlantic, north of Portland Complex and South of Charleston Complex, a somewhat different situation existed. In all of the far North and at Halifax Complex and Montreal Complex, as examples, most of the habitations were intact. The storms were more violent in the north in some respects—the snowfall was eight to ten feet deeper at Montreal Complex—but the tidal waves had done little damage except to dock areas. The buildings in that region were generally sturdy enough to withstand the high winds. South of Charleston Complex the tidal waves were less severe and the principal damage resulted from the winds, for most of the structures in that area were flimsy and not designed to withstand violent weather. In both North and South most of the loss of life resulted from smothering under the snow.

The situation inland was similar. In the Northern Areas and Complexes damage was relatively light. In the South damage was greater. The two great Complexes along the Western Gulf of Mexico were both wiped out completely. There were no more then 500 survivors reported from this area, which had supported some 5,000,000 persons.

The reports from the Pacific Coast were much worse than Gabe Harrow had predicted. The tidal waves had reached unbelievable heights and all of the Complexes, Centers and Cities on the seacoast from Lower California to British Columbia had been obliterated. The loss of life on the West Coast was by far the greatest of any area in the world, with the possible exception of the British Isles (more than 50 per cent inundated) and the North Sea coast from the Channel to Scandinavia. So many millions of persons were lost in the Pacific areas that it is impossible for the imagination to encompass the figures. The destruction was total, for all practical purposes.

This was the overall situation, briefly, on September 27th, 2203.

CHAPTER SIXTEEN

ON FRIDAY just before noon Gabe got a call on the DW-three from Luke Hobson, Secretary for Internal Affairs who explained that he had called at the request of the President who wished to try once more to enlist Gabe's assistance in the great crisis that was engulfing "our nation" and the world.

Gabe, dressed in slacks and a sweater, his face unshaven, smiled engagingly at the Secretary's round face.

"I'm afraid it's too late for any assistance from me," he said. "I told Mr. Gamberelli several months ago, and again as late as the first of September, that all of the seacoast Complexes and Centers on the East and West coasts and the Western Gulf should be evacuated. I was called a variety of names for my trouble. What exactly did you have in mind, Luke?"

"The President wants you to go on the VM and VK and reassure the people," he said. "He believes an encouraging statement from you will do more good at this time than anything any other person could say."

"Encouraging statement," exclaimed Gabe with disgust. "Don't you know that the whole world is freezing up—that there won't be a hundred people left to vote for Alderman unless you organize what's left of the population to survive? And what have you done, beyond declaring a State of Emergency?"

"That's a treasonable attitude at this time of national peril!" exclaimed the Secretary angrily.

"Who's going to get to Fallon to arrest me?"

"This storm will be over soon enough," spluttered Luke Hobson. "We won't forget you, Harrow."

"You won't live to see the day the snow stops," said Gabe quietly. "Don't be an ass, Luke. Tell Mr. Gamberelli—"

The DW-three clicked off suddenly and Gabe was left looking at a blank screen. He turned to me and to Florence and shrugged. He said, "Maybe it's just as well the world will freeze up, with fools like that in it."

On that Friday night around midnight we got a call on the FX Local from the adjoining Lawrence farm. Their house was a 200-year old wood structure, and although it had been renovated several times and expanded to a spacious and attractive farm home, the basic construction had not been strengthened appreciably and certainly not sufficiently to support the tons of snow now weighing down upon their roof. The entire West wing had collapsed, Perry Lawrence told Florence, and he feared the rest of the house would go within hours. Nobody was hurt—fortunately they had all been in bed in the central portion of the house, which was the most sturdy.

Florence told him he would hear from us within a quarter of an hour. She called Gabe on the FX extension in his room, and within five minutes the directors were in the library and considering the Lawrence situation.

Rufe Howard, who had replaced Steve Engles on the board, declared as soon as the situation had been made known that we should organize a rescue team immediately and go get the five Lawrences.

Gabe said, "I'm in favor of that, of course, Rufe, but all of our planning has been for twenty persons. Counting our Arabs, Ali and Sarah, there are now nineteen of us. We could still handle one more without upsetting our balance—but there are five Lawrences. We don't have beds for that many, for one thing."

"Hell, Gabe, you won't know what a bed looks like once we get to the hard part," said Jack Osborne. "The point is only this; we can't abandon them some hundreds of yards away."

"Oh, I agree!" said Gabe. "I just wanted you to know what these five extra ones will mean to us... As a matter of fact, I had intended long before this to propose that we invite the Lawrences to join us. Those two boys Fred and Sam Houston can do ten times the work of us old fogies, and I've always considered Perry and Sylvia my friends."

"Isn't there a girl, too?" I asked. "Seems to me I've heard mention of a Georgia."

"That's the daughter," said Gabe. "We don't talk much about Georgia. You'll see her soon enough and you'll know why."

CHAPTER SEVENTEEN

THE EARLY MORNING of Saturday, September 28th, was the coldest period since the storm's start. The wind had moderated somewhat—to a mere 70 miles an hour—but the temperature had dropped to 30 below zero. The official depth of the snowfall on that date was 18 feet, 5 inches.

Steve Engles and I had been appointed to bring in the Lawrence family. We had both done our year's service in the Antarctic during the second Chinese War—Steve in the Navy and I in the Air Force—and it was the judgment of the directors that this experience equipped us to go the 300 yards to the Lawrence farm.

At the outset of the trek Steve rigged a Cory converter and strapped it to his back while I carried a Bandburger torch and a compass. We could have moved nowhere that night through the wall of snow without a compass. I had laid out a course to the Lawrence front door from a county survey map that, fortunately, was among Gabe's papers.

Ten yards from the Harrow house we encountered a drift at least 50 feet high and we had to crawl off to our left to get around it. Thus I had to chart a new course and I had to do it in my head. Before we had gone fifty yards around the many drifts, my computations had become so complicated that I was taxing my feeble memory to the utmost. All this time we were getting the full force of the snow-filled gale head on. Some of the gusts were easily 90 and 100 miles an hour. It was impossible to move forward against these gusts and we had to lie flat until they passed. Steve would melt a path ahead for several yards and then we would crawl up to the wall of hard-packed snow—almost the consistency of ice. The path would be wet, of course, and the water we picked up on our knees and elbows would freeze before the next few yards of the path could be melted. We could not rest while we waited for the path to be extended or we would have been frozen fast.

Fincham arctics are electronically heated so we were not affected by the cold, but the exertion necessary for forward motion was tremendous. About halfway we had to stop for five minutes and melt the ice from our knees and elbows, which had become too heavy to drag along.

We hit the front porch of the Lawrence farmhouse right on the nose, one hour and 17 minutes after we had left Harrow farm. Steve melted the snow away from the front door and we stumbled into the entry hall, looking more like huge snowballs than men.

Perry and Sylvia Lawrence helped us to de-ice our arctics and we went into the kitchen and drank coffee with the family and discussed our return trip.

Perry and Sylvia were more or less typical of Kansas country people, although better educated than the general run. Perry was a graduate of Kansas Agricultural and had a Master's and Sylvia had attended Western for three years, up to her marriage to Perry. They were both tall and handsome and their strength showed in their faces and in their movements.

The two boys, Fred and Sam Houston, we already knew well, for they had spent much time at Harrow farm the week before helping us to prepare for the storm. Fred was 17 and Sam Houston 18, and they were carbon copies of Perry— already as big as he and almost as strong.

Georgia Lawrence sat at the center of the table, her chin in her hands, looking critically at Steve Engles. She was smaller than her mother, much more delicately built, but she had all of Sylvia's good looks plus an ample share of her father's.

Georgia was what one would term a sultry beauty. She had coal-black hair, blue eyes, and she was quite the sexiest looking girl I had seen since Bali. But on top of all of that there was a strange wildness and decadence about her that was frightening to me. She was 22 and I learned later that she had been married twice, had had one child that had died shortly after birth—some said as a result of mistreatment— and had been involved in a public scandal in York Area One which had been climaxed by the suicide of a prominent and elderly industrialist, who left a widow and four children.

Steve Engles paid no attention to her at first and seemed unaware of her critical examination. Then suddenly—I was talking to Perry at the time and missed the beginning of it— he discovered her. He moved over to sit beside her and he began talking to her in low tones.

Perry agreed with my suggestions on our procedure for return to Harrow farm. Steve was to lead with the converter with Perry behind him with a Bandburger torch, then Sylvia, Sam Houston, Georgia, Fred and myself, bringing up the rear.

We got dressed for the trip, Steve helping Georgia with her jacket and helmet. Steve then doused their reactor and the heat and lights went off. We left by the front door and I closed it carefully after me, being the last one out. I realized it was a useless gesture but I made it anyway.

Steve found our path without difficulty and we started back as we had come, crawling until the strongest gusts hit us, then lying prone until they passed. Going back the wind was at our backs, so forward progress was much easier.

We made the first hundred yards without mishap. Then suddenly, there was a scream, barely audible to me above the howl of the wind. I hurried forward and picked up a huddled mass in the ray of my torch. It was Georgia and Fred and he was trying to pick her up. The others ahead came back and Steve turned down the converter-ray and held it over Georgia. She had her eyes closed, then she opened them and you could see their reflection through the eyeholes in her facemask.

"I'll take care of this," Steve boomed out in a quarterback bellow. He motioned for me to take the converter. He and Perry strapped it on me, then he picked Georgia up as though she were weightless and swung her on his back. She tightened her arms around his neck and we started off once more.

I led the way with the converter and Steve and Georgia came next. Someone with a torch was third, but I didn't bother to check who it was or the order of the others. I used my own torch along with the converter nozzle and I set the fastest pace I could summon up.

We were welcomed back to Harrow farm with an enthusiasm out of all proportion to the simplicity of our feat. Cora was all over Steve, loudly proclaiming his heroism, while the Lawrences were led to the kitchen and plied with hot coffee. Presently most of us were in the kitchen talking to the new members of our group. Georgia came over to Steve, who was standing beside his mother, and said something to them that I didn't hear. Then she put her hand on Steve's face. Cora froze, a look of astonishment in her eyes.

Everyone was suddenly aware of a crisis. The silence was complete and all eyes were turned on the three. Georgia's voice seemed unusually loud as she said, "You saved my life, and I shall never forget you for it. I shall be eternally grateful, Steve." Her "Steve" was in the low, sexy voice of love.

Cora clasped her hand to her bosom and drew in her breath with a sharp cry. "Help me, Steve!" she wailed. "My heart!"

Steve turned to her and led her from the kitchen with a strong arm under her shoulder. Georgia watched their backs, a slight smile playing about her full lips.

CHAPTER EIGHTEEN

EVERY PROJECT of any importance that affected our security had been completed by the end of September, when the snow had reached an official depth of 22 feet. On September 30th the Harrow house was completely covered and the banks on each side of the path we had kept open to the East Barn rose to nearly a hundred feet. By this date we had finished roofing over the path to the East Barn with sheets of Lomax alloy supported on wood beams and we had safe tunnels by which we could move to our storehouse and workshop. The West Barn, which we had abandoned after remaking all of the alloy power tools and other materials of value, collapsed from the weight of the snow on October second.

The only vital continuing activity necessary for our existence was the maintenance of our air vent up through the snow. Bill Wernecke and Ranch Goodrich constructed the tubing from my designs. They used Lomax alloy sheets and pushed the tube to the top of the snow at an angle of 45 degrees. As the snow deepened, additional lengths of tubing were added from the bottom and the whole length pushed up with Corning power jacks. They welded a couple of thousand feet of tubing during the week of September 30th-October 6th and ran through an initial test of the apparatus on October 7th through the bank of snow that had piled up some 120 feet at the rear of the Harrow house. The intake worked perfectly and a great stream of air was sucked into the house by the two fans rigged at the bottom of the pipe. The air had to be heated, of course, so it was diverted to the reactor room where it served the double purpose of cooling the core before it was received into the rest of the house through the heat vents.

On September 30th we had a regular meeting of the directors in the morning and after the several reports by Dr. Howard on health, Jack Osborne on external conditions and Bill Wernecke on the air vent, Gabe Harrow announced that the time had arrived, in his estimation, when all activities would have to be organized and schedules drawn up for the occupation of each member of the group.

"I don't know much about such things," he said apologetically, "but in Einar Crowley's great book on the early Plymouth Platforms, which I've just finished rereading, the commanders found it of prime necessity to organize all activities of their men. Crowley says that even at Plymouth Seven, which was manned entirely by scientists, the boredom brought on bitter quarrels before the daily living was regulated and enforced duties assigned. The resentment against this regimentation was mild and harmless compared to the prior flare-ups. What is your view, Jack Osborne?"

"I agree completely," said Osborne. "We've had somewhat the same problem on Mt. Hood from time to time. Before the present interferometer was completed, and while the old one was out of commission, a dozen of our scientists sat around the Hood Station for three months with nothing to do. During several periods feeling ran very high and physical violence was narrowly averted. I think you are right about your estimate of the time for action, Gabe. All of the novelty of our situation has worn off and most of the fear has evaporated. So we must alter the conditions."

"What do you think, Vic?" asked Gabe.

"I'll go along," I said.

"How about a motion?" he asked.

"Motion is for regimentation along lines to be devised," I said.

"Seconded," said Rufe Howard.

The ayes were unanimous. Gabe said, "Jack Osborne, Bob Jordan and Rufe Howard will draw up assignments and schedules, to be ready tonight. The directors will meet to consider and adopt them at nine P.M. Now what about this situation between Cora Engles and the Lawrence girl?"

"A good question," said Rufe Howard. "I'll tell you this, you've got two women fighting to the death over a man and it isn't very polite."

"Elaine tells me," Gabe said, "that their animosity is beginning to affect the entire group—that sides are being chosen and that we'll all be split right down the middle before the end of the week."

"It's a little over-dramatized," said Bob Jordan. "Libby thinks Cora will capitulate when it's clear Steve and Georgia are serious, and abandon open warfare as soon as they get married. She'll take no chances of losing Steve altogether."

"Georgia Lawrence," said Dr. Howard, "is not in the least interested in marriage. She has used it a couple of times in her pursuit of sensuality, and she's learned as a result that it restricts all her basic impulses and urges, which are essentially sensual and not selective. Now all she wants is sexual variety. The greatest excitement is in getting another woman's man. But once she's got him she will tire of him quickly and start looking about for someone else. I'll give her another month at most with Steve—then watch out. It'll be one of you who's married, you can be certain of that."

"I vote we find her guilty and order her execution forthwith," said Bill Wernecke. "But tell me, Rufe, do you really think she might make a pitch for me?"

"It's all funny now," said Rufe. "Wait another month when our nerves get raw. Let's see what happens then."

"How about a more constructive viewpoint?" Gabe said.

Dr. Howard folded his hands over his plump middle and nodded his gray head. "I presume my medical degree makes it incumbent upon me to prescribe," he said. "I can think of nothing better to offer than the isolation of Cora and Georgia from each other. How you will achieve that in this limited community, I am at a loss to suggest."

"Give it some thought," said Gabe, "when you and Jack and Bob draw up the activities assignments. You've got twenty-four hours in each day and it isn't necessary for all of us to be up and about during the same periods."

CHAPTER NINETEEN

AT DINNER on Monday night, September 30th, there occurred the first display of general hostility since we had gathered as a group. We were eating fresh food from the Harrow freezer, and the night's fare was roast of beef, potatoes and cauliflower.

Perry Lawrence said, "An excellent roast, done to a turn."

Steve Engles, who was sitting close by with Georgia, agreed. Georgia said, "I like mine a little less done. Rare meat for me."

Cora Engles turned to Florence Donner beside her and said loudly enough for all to hear, "She's never even learned to boil water, but she presumes to criticize *my* cooking!"

Georgia jumped to her feet and upset her plate on the floor (we were eating buffet style). "Keep that old crone off my neck or I'll kill her!" she shouted.

"Old crone!" echoed Cora hysterically. "Stevie, are you going to stand for such vile insults to your mother?"

Steve sat looking from Georgia to Cora. Then he took Georgia's hand.

Martha Wernecke, who should have had better sense, said, "Cora is right. After all, she *did* cook the roast."

Bill Wernecke said to her, "Shut up, Martha. You don't belong in this."

Martha turned on him furiously. "You would side with that cheap little girl!" she exclaimed.

Bill's reply was lost in the general bedlam that burst suddenly upon us, husbands and wives yelling at each other, Gabe demanding quiet, Georgia now in a tantrum and smashing every plate she could get her hands on, Cora calling for Stevie to defend her, and Alice Wernecke screaming hysterically in the fear of a ten-year-old.

Marge clung tightly to my arm. "Keep out of it," she said in my ear. "You can't do anything but make it worse."

"Go over and slap Georgia," I said. "That'll bring her around. She's hysterical."

"You slap her," replied Marge. "You're bigger than I am."

"Then I'll have to slap Steve, too, and that won't be healthy for either of us," I said.

Marge let go of my arm and moved quickly to Georgia's side. She swung her around by a shoulder and slapped her a resounding blow on the side of the face.

The surprise of it stopped all sound except the wailing of Alice. Then Alice quieted, too, and everyone watched the scene in the center of the room. Steve started to move angrily towards the two girls. Marge took Georgia in her arms and patted her head affectionately.

"I'm sorry I did that to you, darling," she said in a cooing voice, as though speaking to a child. "I had to—you were hysterical. Come on upstairs and lie down in my room. I'll get you some coffee."

Marge led Georgia out of the living room. The rest of us stood about looking at each other. We were all too embarrassed to say anything. Finally Elaine spoke up, standing at Gabe's side.

"As your hostess, I invite you all to resume dinner," she said. "Personally, I think Cora did a beautiful job of cooking it."

Rance Goodrich laughed, then we all laughed. In that instant tension was broken and we were once more a civilized group of friends.

Even Cora joined in the mirth, although her laughter was hardly hearty. She told Steve her heart was bothering her and asked him to help her to her room.

Gabe said, "I think we're all getting a little stir-crazy. Tomorrow I'll have a schedule for everyone. Please report to me in the library at eight A.M. Class dismissed, delinquents."

His announcement was greeted by cheers, and our spirits remained up for the rest of the evening. On that night, right after dinner, Rance Goodrich organized the first Bridge game.

At the meeting of the directors that followed dinner, we spent an hour discussing and approving the assignments of duties for the company. Cora was assigned as chief cook three days a week, with full responsibility for the menus (Elaine and Sylvia Lawrence shared this position the other four) and on Friday, Saturday, Sunday, and Monday Cora was housekeeper, responsible for laundry, mending, cleaning, etc. Georgia was assigned as communications monitor from midnight to 8:00 A.M. seven days a week and she was given three weeks to become proficient in the Albee and Morse codes. We fondly hoped that these assignments would keep Cora and Georgia apart—and also keep Georgia working or sleeping most of the hours when the rest of us were up and about.

I was named vice commander of the Harrow Group under Gabe and was given the responsibility of overseeing all of the assignments and enforcing the work schedules. The directors insisted, and my lone nay carried no weight.

We set up various work details to keep all of our equipment and tools in order and we organized schools as well to teach all the members of our group the various skills in which some of us were proficient. Bill Wernecke was assigned to conduct an electronics school, Steve Engles was to hold classes on reactor techniques, I was to conduct a class in navigation, and a general elementary school was set up for Alice and Tony Wernecke, with Marge as Schoolmarm.

We adjourned our meeting, and at 1:00 A.M. I started on a tour of the house and the barn, in accordance with my new responsibilities. I found nothing in the house that needed attention and then I walked out through our new tunnel. I found the East Barn dark and my first thought was that a tube had burned out. I put on my flashlight and moved toward the switch panel to light an alternate tube. Steve's voice from out of the darkness to my left said, "Don't turn on any lights, Vic."

I was startled, of course. Steve was the last person I expected to be in the barn, with his mother in the throes of a heart attack. So I asked the inevitable silly question...

"That you, Steve?"

"Yes. Go back to the house. Everything's okay here."

I turned towards the door, then stopped.

"You alone?" I asked him.

"No," he replied.

So I went back to the house.

The next morning, Tuesday, October first, at 7:10 Cora Engles was found dead in her bed by Steve, who had gone to her room with coffee to awaken her.

CHAPTER TWENTY

IT IS DIFFICULT to assay the effect that Cora's death had on the Harrow Group. There was little outward manifestation of grief or even shock, except in the case of Steve and, unexpectedly, Sylvia Lawrence...perhaps Sylvia more surely than the rest of us understood why Cora had died.

When Steve had determined that his mother was dead and not asleep, and cried out his dismay, Florence Donner, who occupied the adjoining bedroom, came running in. She sounded a general light-alarm almost immediately (alarm buttons had been rigged in every room) and Gabe, Elaine and I were the next to respond. Dr. Howard was along seconds later.

Steve was on his knees by the bed, his head resting on his mother's still bosom. I took him by the arm and he rose to his feet. I led him from the room and downstairs and he sat in front of the fireplace, looking at the dead coals.

I tried to get him to talk but he would say nothing.

Georgia came downstairs in a pale blue dressing gown with narrow black fur around the collar and went to the other side of Steve's chair. She stood looking at him for a moment, then looked up at me. "What's all the excitement about?" she asked, motioning upstairs.

"It's Steve's mother," I said. "She's dead."

Georgia's face was as blank as Steve's. She nodded her head a couple of times, then put a hand on Steve's shoulder. "I'm sorry," she said.

He raised his eyes to hers. "It happened last night while we were—out there," he said.

"Well—I'm sorry." The "well" was almost belligerent.

"That's when it happened—last night," he said. "I should have known it would."

"I'm damned!" exclaimed Georgia. She swung around and ran back to the stairs and up.

Steve turned to look at me for the first time. There was no grief in his eyes, just anger.

"What the hell's got into her?" he demanded.

"Whatever it is, it'll blow over," I said. "How about some coffee, Steve?"

He shook his head and resumed his staring at the fireplace.

Rufe Howard and Gabe came down the stairs and motioned to me to come with them into the library. Gabe closed the door as Rufe and I sat.

"What's the verdict, Rufe?" he asked, pacing between the door and the table.

"Looks like lacatine to me," said Rufe. "Dead about five hours, I would guess."

"Suicide?" asked Gabe.

"If it's lacatine, then she took them herself," he replied. "One of those pills of hers would kill a roomful, and she could have taken one by mistake in the dark. They're the same shape and size as those so-called heart pills she takes."

"Why would she commit suicide?" Gabe demanded.

"It all ties in with my dissertation on Georgia Lawrence," said Rufe Howard. "You may remember that I said then we had two women fighting to the death over a man. I didn't know how prophetic I was being, heaven help me. If I'd just thought this through a little further, I might have been able to do something about it. So now Cora's dead. And do you know why she's dead? Because by her death she evens the score. Not with Georgia—she never gave a damn about her—but with son Steve. This is the greatest possible punishment she could inflict upon him for his disloyalty to her—for his desertion of her for another woman.

"Cora's been having a heart attack every night since Saturday and the arrival of the Lawrences and I was under the impression Steve was spending his nights with her."

"Not last night," I said. "Sometime after one A.M. he was down at the East Barn."

"Alone?" asked Gabe.

"He said he was not alone," I replied.

"Then we'd better call it accident," said Gabe. "It'll save Steve's feelings that way, but more importantly, it will deprive Georgia of a victory. Frankly, I'd be a little afraid of such a victory for Georgia in our confined community."

CHAPTER TWENTY-ONE

THE TREK to the Lawrence farm was the last sortie any of us made from Harrow farm for the duration of the deep cold, which lasted for the next three months. During October, November and December, the temperature never rose above 30 below zero, and for the last week in November and the first in December it hovered around 45 below. The gales continued at velocities between 70 and 90 miles per hour, and during the two weeks of deepest cold the wind force on several occasions reached over 100 miles per hour.

There was no letup in the precipitation, of course, and in the 96 days to January first, 2204, approximately 160 feet of snow fell over the Northern Hemisphere, according to official reports. The R.N.A. Weather Bureau at Chicago Complex continued to function up to March 16th and sent out daily reports over UHF as well as the VM and VK while the latter circuits continued in operation. The Chicago Bureau was, fortunately, situated in the fabulous Corning Tower, which rose some 1,200 feet above Lake Michigan.

In the vicinity of Fallon the official depth of the snow on the first of the year was 175 feet, 4 inches. But these official depths had little meaning for us. At Harrow farm the snow had piled up to well over 200 feet and our air vent pipe extended more than 300 feet to the top of the snow. The bottom layers of the snow had been compressed to solid ice, to a depth of five or six feet, and it was this ice that was to prove the greatest danger to us, as it thickened.

Under Gabe Harrow's direction we had constructed a wood bay just outside the front porch of the farmhouse so that we could keep track of the thickness of the ice and the consistency of the snow to a height of 50 feet. When the ice got thick enough so that its weight over a large area would overcome friction, then it would start to move—in the direction of lower ground, of course. This was the glacial action that was to be expected, and the one phenomena that we would have no way of resisting. When the ice started to move, we would have to abandon Harrow farm, no matter what the conditions were on the surface.

Both the VM and VK stations went off the air the middle of December, and our only communication with the outside world thereafter was by old-fashioned VHF and UHF. Most of the reports on these frequencies were in Albee or Morse code, but both Florence Donner and Georgia Lawrence had become proficient in receiving code, so we remained operational. We still had the DW-three, but at Gabe's orders it had been put on "emergency out" since his encounter with Luke Hobson.

"The DW-three system will collapse soon enough anyway, along with all the rest of their gadgets," Gabe said. "I'll be much surprised if they have anything in Government functioning after the first of the year outside of their new electronic toilets."

Life at Harrow farm had settled quickly into a fixed routine and, like any routine, it was the acme of dullness. Any new games quickly became old games and as boring as those we had abandoned. There was no way to combat the dullness except to withdraw into oneself and avoid as much awareness of the external world as was possible.

All of us from the two Wernecke children up to Rufe Howard, the oldest of the group, began to show the wear of our incarceration as the end-of-December storms reached their height. The most affected were Georgia Lawrence and Steve Engles.

Georgia found no satisfactory outlet for her erotic urges among the males of our community, though she came close just once. Of our bachelors, Rance Goodrich, the most eligible, had become enamored of redheaded Florence Donner and didn't know Georgia existed. Jack Osborne was impervious to the obvious charms that were displayed for his benefit and continually aroused Georgia's anger by treating her as a backward child. Dr. Howard, of course, was immune to her, and Steve was the discarded lover who had served his purpose and was no longer acceptable.

Georgia made her greatest effort towards Bob Jordan.

Libby Jordan told me that she believed it started early on the morning of November 12th, when Bob was called to the communications room to repair the main UHF receiver, which had developed a short circuit. She thought it was peculiar at the time that he should have been summoned, because the radio repair work normally was done by Fred or

Sam Houston Lawrence. But she forgot about it and went back to sleep. She woke up a couple of hours later when the heated blanket became too warm and Bob was not back in bed yet. She checked the time. It was 3:30 A.M. He came back to their bedroom finally at 4:10 A.M. She asked him what had been keeping him and he said, "That Georgia. I was listening to her prattle. She's a smart little girl about some things."

"About sex?" Libby asked.

"Yes, I guess she knows about that, too," he said, "but we were talking about psychology. She's got a good foundation in that."

Bob was up late for the next two nights, giving Libby no explanation other than that he couldn't sleep, and on the morning of November 15th Libby sought me out in the library where I was doing my Friday morning bookkeeping on snow and ice figures, length of vent, tonnages of stores and states of the various structures. Libby said, "I want to talk to you. You'll probably want to take this up with Gabe, but I'm going to tell you because I can talk to you easier. It has nothing to do with me personally, although it may sound so—but what I am mainly concerned with is the position of all of us and not my own little problem. It's Bob and Georgia."

"What about them?" I asked.

"Bob's just about to have an affair with her. He's right on the brink and if I know her, she'll give him the necessary shove the next time they get together. That will probably be tonight. Look, Vic, I've been married to Bob for eight years and he's a hell of a guy, but he wouldn't be able to resist Georgia's offerings under these conditions. He just can't put up with this boredom as well as some of us can, and he's got to find some outlet for his energies if he has to pull the whole house down around our necks. That's exactly what he'll do if he gets any deeper with this girl. He'll fall in love with her surely—and then, when she starts hunting around for someone else; he'll kill her. Vic, it's got to be stopped right away!"

I went to see Gabe and Elaine in their room. I was just finishing my account of the situation when the light alarm went on for the East Barn. We put on our arctics, and ran through the tunnel to the barn.

Fred Lawrence was standing by the alarm button, his face white with fear. Facing each other near the workbench to the right of the door were Bob Jordan and Steve Engles. Jordan had a gash on his forehead and blood was streaming down his face. He was holding a Cory converter nozzle in his hands, pointed at Steve. Engles, a wild look in his eyes and his shoulders hunched forward, was glaring at Bob and moving a wood club in his right hand as though he were going to swing it regardless of the deadly converter.

I hurried over, grabbed Steve's arm and took the club away from him. He turned on me with fury and swung a fist at my head. I stepped in close and threw him. I held him down by the arms and Bob dropped the converter and came over to help.

"What happened?" I asked him.

"He's blown his top," Bob replied. "He whacked me with that club and I think he would have killed me if I hadn't got the converter."

Gabe brought me a length of small drinal cord and I tied Steve's wrists and arms. Then I got off his back and he sat up slowly. He appeared to be dazed.

"Do you want to go back to the house?" I asked him.

He looked at me for a long moment, then his eyes suddenly seemed to focus. "What?" he asked.

I repeated the question.

"Sure," he said. "Why'd you tie me up?"

"You tried to kill Bob Jordan," I said.

"Untie me," he said. "I'm all right now." He nodded to Bob. "I'm sorry," he told him. "I don't know what came over me."

I untied the cord and Steve got to his feet. Gabe asked him, "Why did you attack Bob, Steve?"

"I guess I was upset about Georgia."

"About Georgia and Bob Jordan?" Elaine asked. She had washed off the blood from Bob's head and face and was bandaging the wound from an emergency kit.

Steve looked around at each one of us before replying. "When I saw them together last night I went all to pieces. I felt myself slipping down—I can't describe it!"

"When you saw us together!" exclaimed Bob. "My God, man, I was only talking to the girl!"

"You were alone with her," Steve said. "I know how she is when you're alone with her."

"I don't think Bob would give up someone like Libby for a girl like Georgia," I said.

"What's the matter with Georgia?" demanded Steve.

"Nothing," I said, "but she doesn't compare to Libby in looks or in any other way. Let's face the facts, Steve."

"I guess you're right," he said. "I've just got to get over that damned Georgia and get my sanity back. Look at the mess I've made!"

We all started back to the house. I dropped behind the others with Bob Jordan. I said, "You're the one who's making a mess, Bob. Leave Georgia alone."

"But I haven't touched her!" he exclaimed.

"Perhaps, but how long do you think Georgia will keep her hands off you if she thinks you like her?"

He was silent for a few steps. Then he said, "You know, Vic, you were right back there about Libby."

And that ended that.

CHAPTER TWENTY-TWO

WE WERE SO DEEP under the snow on Christmas that we were entirely unaware of the storm that raged far above. However, our thermometers and wind gauges rigged to the top of our air vent told us that the gale had increased and the temperature had dropped.

A short service was held at midnight, conducted by Gabe for the benefit of the two Wernecke children, we said. But I think it was for the benefit of all of us. Georgia Lawrence was the only member of the group who did not attend. Steve wept unashamedly all through it.

Afterwards Rufe Howard warned Gabe and me that there were definite signs Steve was nearing an emotional crackup. He explained in detail the effects of his mother's death and his unhappy affair with Georgia, and he declared his withdrawal had now reached the point where he might at any moment become a danger to himself and possibly to others.

"There is no way in the world," Rufe said, "that we can predict what channels his mind will follow, but I strongly urge that he be kept under surveillance. I'm going to put him on drugs beginning tonight and see if I can't alleviate his condition."

"I'll alert the company to keep an eye on him," Gabe said. "Perhaps we can bar his door at night so he won't go roving about."

"How's Georgia getting along since Bob Jordan abandoned her?" I asked.

Rufe shook his head. "She's not well at all, Vic. That Jordan incident didn't do her morale any good. She's like a reactor boiler with eight hundred pounds of steam and no place to let it off. She's taken to confiding in me. My colleagues of the unenlightened Twentieth Century described a personality that seems to fit her exactly. They called this one a C.P.I., for constitutional psychopathic inferior, and the high points are, briefly, exaggerated self-dramatization, alternations of elation and depression, an inability to sustain love, egomania, and lack of moral standards."

"What happens when this little bundle of dynamite blows up?" Gabe asked.

"She won't blow up," said Rufe. "She's got a built-in safety valve that will let her go just so far and no farther. Georgia, my friends, is going to be with us a long time."

"Unless some one of us does her in," I said.

Our Christmas dinner was turkey and all the trimmings, cooked by Sylvia Lawrence. We had saved out four frozen birds from the last of our fresh supplies for the occasion and our dinner at the bottom of the snow was a gala affair. Everyone including Georgia entered into the spirit of the occasion, and for nearly three hours on that Christmas day we were normal human beings again with regard and consideration for each other and no boredom to fray our nerves and sink us to despair.

Marge was her old self, a lighthearted and amusing companion, and we sat near the fireplace with our plates on our laps and chatted like olden times. But perhaps I do Marge an injustice. To be honest, I must admit that our imprisonment had had little effect upon her disposition and that nearly all of the strain in our relationship had come from my own restlessness and resentment of the confinement and routine.

Because Marge was a woman of many facets and skills and completely self-reliant, I wondered many times why it had taken me so long to discover her priceless attitudes. She organized, admonished, advised and was in the forefront of all general activities, whether games or work.

Her classes for Alice and Anthony Wernecke proved so enjoyable to the two children that word spread, and soon they were being attended from time to time by Rance Goodrich, Bob and Libby Jordan, Fred Lawrence and occasionally by

Gabe and Elaine. I sat in on a couple of them to see what was going on and I was fascinated by her presentation of history, which was done with a humor and good sense that would have been a revelation to the textbook writers.

CHAPTER TWENTY-THREE

OUR CELEBRATION of the New Year, which we had looked forward to with so much anticipation after the success of our Christmas dinner, developed into a wake rather than a fete.

Up at the top of the snow the wind was howling at more than 100 miles per hour and the temperature was steady at 45 degrees below zero. At Harrow farm, 200 feet below the weather, we were warm, comfortable, and restless. At 6:00 P.M. on Tuesday, the last day of the year, we gathered in the living room and drank Martinis mixed by Ali. I went into the kitchen to find out what Ali had put in them and was met by a local storm of no small proportions. Martha Wernecke and Sylvia Lawrence were having a ring-around with Ali and Sarah, apparently over the pot washing and kitchen straightening, and all four were screaming at each other. I tried to get them calmed down with no success. I went back to the living room and sent Elaine in to handle it.

The cocktail hour was a flop. The liquor, which was served only on special occasions such as this, seemed to have a depressing effect upon all of us.

The dinner, of food concentrates but tastefully prepared by Martha and Sylvia and served on gaily decorated platters, was eaten in morose silence for the most part.

After dinner most of the company started to drink bourbon highballs. I spoke to Gabe Harrow about the growing tension and my fears of a brawl some time around 11:00 P.M.

"It'll do most of us more good than harm to tie one on," Gabe replied. "They'll all be sorry in the morning, but tonight's what counts right now."

At 11:30 the first fight broke out—between Steve Engles and Perry Lawrence. There was no clear account of what started it. The two had encountered each other in the hallway leading to the kitchen, Perry on his way to check on Martha, and Steve coming out of the washroom off the hall. Perry either did or did not make a disparaging remark to Steve. He denied it but both Steve and Florence Donner said they heard it.

Steve's reply was bitter and Perry hit him in the nose with his fist. Florence called loudly for me but before I could get there Steve had thrown Perry and was sitting on his back and pounding his head.

I pulled Steve off and ordered Perry to vanish. Steve was angry but controlled. For a moment it appeared that he would swing on me next, but he resisted that impulse and apologized instead.

"He shouldn't have hit me, but I shouldn't have thrown him either," he said rationally. "I guess I don't belong among the snowbound tonight, Vic. I'll go up to my room and get some sleep, if Doc Howard will give me a pill."

Georgia came into the hall and stood regarding Steve with animosity.

"You're a big, strong bully-boy," she said sarcastically. "Why don't you try hitting me?"

"I thought you hated your father," Steve said.

"That's none of your business," she replied, coloring at his revelation of a confidence. "You've got no right to hit people!"

"Perry's as big as I am," said Steve. "What's the matter with you, Georgia? Why do you want to fight with me?"

"You go to hell!" she said. "You can all go to hell!" She ran back to the living room.

Steve started after her. "I'm going to find out what's the matter with her," he said.

I went into the kitchen to check on the chores there and to invite Sarah and Ali to have a midnight drink with all of us. Sarah was sitting at the table, her head in her arms and sobbing as though her heart was breaking. Ali was standing near the sink waving a frying pan and wailing a tuneless oriental song. Both of them were as drunk as Space tourists.

As I re-entered the living room the second fight had just broken out, between Rance Goodrich and Bob Jordan. Bill Wernecke and Jack Osborne were moving in fast and each had hold of a combatant by the time I reached them. Neither Bob nor Rance needed a peacemaker; each was too drunk to make any sense or listen to any, and neither had the slightest notion what he was fighting about. They staggered away with their arms about each other's shoulders.

Marge said to me, "What are you so glum about? You want to get into a fight, too?"

"No, darling," I replied. "But I *am* depressed."

"Let's have a drink together. It's just about midnight."

We filled two glasses with sherry and toasted each other and the New Year. Then there was whistling and yelling and a group started to sing Auld Lang Syne. It was twelve o'clock. I took Marge in my arms and kissed her long and tenderly, and I told her that I loved her.

At around 1:00 A.M. she said she wanted to go up to bed and I walked upstairs with her. I told her I would join her as soon as the party conked out and kissed her good night. On my way down I met Rufe Howard at the head of the stairs. I asked him if he'd seen Steve and if he'd given him a sleeping pill.

He shook his head. "Not since dinner," he said. "Let's see if he's in his room."

We went to Steve's room near the stairs and knocked. There was no answer. Rufe tried the door and it opened.

There on the bed lay Steve and Georgia, clothed, locked in each other's arms, sound asleep.

Rufe and I backed out, and Rufe closed the door softly.

"What do you make of that, Doctor?" I asked.

"It wouldn't figure at all for normal people," he said. "For those two, anything could happen. I suppose she just had no choice. Her confidence must have been badly shaken by that Bob Jordan affair, so she's had to take what's available... Well, here we go again."

He went down the hall to his own room, which was next to Marge's and mine, and I went back downstairs.

Young Fred Lawrence told me there had been two more fights but neither had amounted to anything. He was sitting on the bottom step, watching the antics of his elders as though he were at a play.

I checked in the kitchen and Ali and Sarah were not in sight. I assumed they had retired to their room adjoining the kitchen. I took a tour of the tunnel and the East Barn instead and I found nothing amiss except a slight potential hazard to the equanimity of some of us. Libby Jordan and Jack Osborne were sitting together on the workbench, Jack's arm around Libby, in confidential conversation. They were both quite tight and they greeted me boisterously.

I said, "I presume you two came out here to talk."

Libby laughed gaily. "That's all Jack's been doing," she said. "I brought him out here to seduce him but this is as far as I've got."

"You wouldn't try to seduce me!" exclaimed Osborne. "That's the tragedy of my life—that I'm in love with you and you pay me no heed."

We three walked back together through the tunnel and I left them in the hall. The living room was nearly cleared—there were only Bill Wernecke and Perry Lawrence, in earnest conversation near the fireplace. I checked on the communications room and found Florence Donner there monitoring the UHF and VHF, with Rance Goodrich asleep in a deep chair.

"You sitting in for Georgia tonight?" I asked her.

"She'll be down after a while," Florence replied. "She was getting her libido adjusted. I bet we have some more fireworks, Vic."

"I know," I said. "Let's not block the exits when the panic starts."

I went up to bed.

At 4:10 A.M. I was awakened by a scream from Florence Donner's room. I got in there in seconds and found myself suddenly pinned from behind by a person of great strength. There was a sharp pain in my side and I grabbed a hand with a knife in it.

I threw the man off my back, kicked him hard in the head, then turned on the light. On the floor lay Ali Bed Douka, unconscious, with a long, bloodstained kitchen knife near his open right hand. On the bed, still breathing but unconscious, was Florence Donner, with a frightful slash from her head down to her left breast. On the floor on the other side of the bed, dressed in trousers and shirt, was the body of Rance Goodrich, dead. There was a knife wound just above his heart, and his shirtfront was covered with blood.

Rufe Howard came in then with several others from the guest wing. Rufe took a fast look at Rance, then went to work immediately on Florence. I went back to Ali and started to bend over to pick him up when I saw that I was leaking, too, from my right side.

I told Bill Wernecke, "Get the Arab downstairs and tied up. He went berserk. Check on everybody, Bill. God knows where he's been before he got in here. Check on Sarah, too. It'll be a wonder if she's alive."

Bill carried Ali out and I sat in a chair and looked at the bloody knife, waiting for Rufe Howard to get to me. I wasn't in any pain but I began to feel awfully weak. Maybe five minutes elapsed before I passed out.

CHAPTER TWENTY-FOUR

CRAZED ALI KILLED Rance Goodrich, Elaine Harrow and his wife Sarah on the bloody morning of January 1. He wounded Gabe Harrow severely—just missing his heart by a fraction of an inch—and Florence Donner and, less seriously, myself.

We believe that his mind became unbalanced and that sometime after 2:00 A.M. he killed his wife. He butchered her body with the precision with which he would have butchered a calf, draining the blood into the bathtub and washing it down with water.

Then he started on his tour of the house, apparently bent upon killing us all. He went first to the Harrow bedroom on the first floor, killed Elaine and stabbed Gabe. Georgia, in the communications room two walls away, heard nothing. She had a headpiece over her ears at that time, so it was not surprising. Steve had been with her up to 2:00 A.M. and he said he saw no one nor heard anything on his way back to his bedroom.

Ali then went upstairs and down our hall. Why he picked Florence Donner's room first was anybody's guess. Probably he selected it at random, not concerned who was within as long as it was some member of our company for him to kill.

On the following morning the directors considered the case of Ali Ben Douka. Gabe presided. His wound had proved superficial, but he was listless and inattentive.

I read off the results of my investigation, and then asked Gabe what he proposed we should do about it.

"I don't know," he said. "What do you all think? Rufe?"

"We can't keep Ali locked in the barn," said Rufe, "We have to use the barn. He wouldn't be safe anywhere in the house. There are no locks on any of the doors and I wouldn't want him that close to me anyway. I'm afraid we haven't much choice."

"Is he sane now?" asked Bill Wernecke.

Rufe shrugged. "He may be and he may not be. He appears sane but he has no remorse for his blood bath and he refuses to answer questions. I'm frank to say I can't handle him, gentlemen."

Jack Osborne said, "I think our only course is to dispose of this man. We are not in a position to do anything else and the safety of the group is our only consideration here."

Gabe nodded. "What do you want to do, Vic?" he asked.

"I think we'd better vote on it," I said.

I framed a resolution calling for the execution of Ali Ben Douka. The ayes were unanimous.

"All right," I said. "I'll take care of it."

The meeting was adjourned and I went out to the East Barn.

CHAPTER TWENTY-FIVE

WE HELD SERVICES for our New Year's dead on the following day, Friday. Burial was just off the tunnel near the barn where we melted a hole back into the ice just below the snow line. Gabe did not attend the service. He had remained in his room since the meeting of the directors.

"I don't seem to be able to summon the will to get out of this chair," he told me. "I don't think I could face those remains of Elaine without breaking down, and that wouldn't be of any help to any of you. You run things, Vic. It was never a job for me and now it's doubly unacceptable without Elaine. She gave me my strength."

He fell silent, his eyes cast down, his chin in his hands. I walked to the door and closed it quietly after me.

When we had returned to the house after the service, I passed the word to Jack Osborne, Bob Jordan, Bill Wernecke and Rufe Howard that there would be a meeting of the directors immediately. The five of us gathered in the library. Rufe asked if Gabe would join us.

"No," I replied. "That's what this meeting is about. Gabe told me before the service that he was withdrawing from direction of the group unless we needed him. He told me that I was to take over in his place. But it is up to the board to decide whom this will be. I should like to nominate Rufe Howard."

"No, no!" exclaimed Rufe. "I am not fitted for such a position by training or inclination."

"Let's vote on the selection of Victor Savage," Bill Wernecke said. "I nominate him."

"Seconded," said Rufe.

The vote was taken and I was appointed. I said, "I accept this appointment upon one condition. It is that if and when Gabe Harrow wishes to resume leadership, he shall do so with our unanimous approval."

The directors accepted.

Jack Osborne said, "We give you a lot of power, Vic. I mention this not because I am afraid you will misuse it, but because I want to urge a firmer hand on the controls than Gabe has given us. Five of us have died in the first three months of our imprisonment. Let's have no more of this."

I looked around at the four intense faces and I pointed a finger at Bill Wernecke. "Bill?" I demanded.

He thought for a moment, then answered, "Jack's right in a way, but I wouldn't blame Gabe for anything that's happened to any of us so far. Maybe if five more of us die in the next three months, then I'll have something to say to you. Right now I would second the motion that you are responsible for the lives of all of us."

"You want to add anything, Rufe?" I asked Dr. Howard.

He nodded. "I felt that I messed up this situation with Cora Engles. Also that if I had been more astute, I might have foreseen the crackup of Ali. It is easy to blame one's self after the fact, however, just as it is now quite reasonable to blame Gabe... Give us all hell, my boy, and see if you can make us behave so that we'll live to regret it."

I looked at Bob Jordan and he shook his head. "Just get us out of this, that's all," he said.

I inaugurated immediately a set of regulations, and I appointed Bob Jordan, Perry Lawrence, and Bill Wernecke as provosts to enforce them. There was to be no more drinking of whiskey or other spirits. Work hours were to be strictly observed, as were the hours of recreation. There was to be no quarreling, all disputes to be settled by myself. In any matters affecting individuals and not the group, an appeal could be taken from my decisions to the directors. In matters affecting the group, there was no appeal: my word was the law.

Punishments for violations were set up. Minor violations brought extra chores, including the time-honored K.P. Major violations brought isolation from the group for varied periods, according to the gravity of the offense.

As it was, the Regulations were accepted as a matter of course—possibly as just another irritation among the innumerable ones of our restricted life.

CHAPTER TWENTY-SIX

WE HAD no more difficulties with Steve Engles after his New Year's Eve outburst and he very quickly regained much of his old balance and confidence. I have no doubt that his reconciliation with Georgia had more to do with it than any of the medication from Rufe Howard, although it is hardly possible that their relationship could have been very satisfactory to either. They were both extremely discreet and avoided each other at most public gatherings. We all knew that they were spending much time together in Steve's room—it would hardly have been possible for them to have hidden this in such a small community—but there was surprisingly little discussion of them or their affair except between the Wernecke children, who were openly fascinated by it.

The effect of the reconciliation upon Georgia was not at all what I would have expected, although Rufe Howard said she was reacting in the expected way. She seemed more morose and dissatisfied than ever and her temper was short with most of us and particularly so with Bob Jordan, Jack Osborne and me. In my case, she was seldom civil, except to be deliberately provocative or suggestive. She never missed an opportunity to try to embarrass me in front of others.

During all of January and most of February our depressed state was constant. Our fresh food supplies had run out in November; we were on food-concentrates. On February 25th we discovered the first glacier-movement of the ice mantle that rested on the ground, and this news, bad as it was from one standpoint, broke our deep depression and raised our spirits and activity both to a level where they remained for the rest of our imprisonment.

This day saw the ice reach a thickness of thirty-two feet at the measuring bay. At Gabe Harrow's suggestion, we had rigged a pressure meter there, attached to the foundations of the farmhouse. It showed twenty-five pounds of pressure per square inch on this day, which was the first positive reading the gauge had given.

I called a meeting of the directors immediately—this was at 9:15 A.M.—and the matter was discussed with animation.

Bill Wernecke said the pressure would not become dangerous until it reached thousands of pounds. He recommended hourly readings and said we should be able to tell within twenty-four hours just how much time we had before we would have to abandon Harrow farm.

The idea of leaving our haven under the snow was a frightening one, yet it was that idea that gave us new zest. The prospect of going out on top to fight our way to the sea through the boundless snowscape fired our imaginations and made us heedless of the dangers.

On this 25th day of February, 2204, the snow had piled up more than 500 feet above us, undoubtedly due to drifting. The official snowfall on that date, according to the Chicago Complex Bureau, was 325 feet. This figure was of academic interest only, for the Bureau admitted that all actual measurements reported were far greater than 325 feet. The temperature had risen to around ten below zero and the wind had died to a mere 70-90 miles per hour.

I called Florence Donner into the meeting to give us the last-minute reports on the weather, and particularly those in the Equatorial area. Florence had recovered quickly from the slashing by Ali, which was not nearly as bad as it had first appeared. She still wore bandages on her face and neck but Rufe Howard had reported there would be no noticeable scars. He had used the new Fogarthy Clinic technique in treating her wounds. But she had not recovered at all from Rance Goodrich's death and she made her report in a voice that was as lifeless as an electronic pickup.

She told us that the latest reports of Equatorial temperatures, which had come in the night before, ranged from ten degrees below zero at sea level to 30 degrees below in the high mountains. She said that reports from two stations, at Freetown in Africa and at Pernambuco were of winds at 65 miles per hour. Snowfall was averaging about 19 inches per 24 hours.

After Florence had left, I asked Jack Osborne about the possibility of our immediate movement to the sea and thence South, so far as it concerned the weather.

"I'd rather talk to Gabe before giving you an opinion," he said. "But I'll tell you this, I was with him last night and he told me that he would consider it foolhardy for us to think of moving out of here for another four months."

I said, "We'll move out when we have to, Jack. I propose that in anticipation of our movement we assemble the snow-mobile and begin the construction of a tunnel-ramp up to the surface."

"I'd want Gabe's opinion," said Jack Osborne.

"Not on this," I said. "It is our agreement, and our regulations provide that on such matters I have the final and only say. My reasoning is simply that I am not going to endanger our lives by reposing confidence in the movements of a glacier. It may move very slowly, but if by some freak it should speed up and we were caught without a proper escape route, we would all die."

Rufe Howard said, "It'll give us all something different to do and I'm in favor of that. You go ahead and issue your orders, boy, and I'll give Jack Osborne a pill to quiet him down if he tries to get in your way."

I assigned Bill Wernecke to take the readings on the pressure gauge and adjourned the meeting. Osborne stayed in the library after the others had left and he told me, "I don't mean to question your judgment or your authority. I'll just have to learn to keep my cautious ways to myself...You tell me what you want me to do."

I told him I wanted him to talk to Gabe and see if he could find any safe basis for our moving east sooner than four months. "Tell Gabe we can't wait that long," I said.

I went into the communications room to see Florence and to try to cheer her up. She was sitting over a table with earphones on and her head resting on an arm. Her eyes were closed. Georgia Lawrence was asleep in a deep chair in a corner. I sat down across the table from Florence and poked her arm.

"You've got to stop mourning Rance Goodrich," I said. "Life has got to go on without him."

"Not my life," said Florence, raising her head slowly and looking at me. "I don't care about living."

"You've got to care," I said harshly. "Not for yourself but for the others. If you funk out, you're going to carry some of them with you and then maybe none of us will survive. This at the bottom of the snow is nothing compared with what we are going to face when we get on top. We need you alive and fighting alongside the rest of us."

She had removed a receiver from one ear to hear me. Now she took the headset off and placed it gently on the table.

"I'll try, Vic," she said. "I hadn't realized about the others." I got up and patted her shoulder. "Do me a favor," I said. "Make a pitch for Jack Osborne. He needs someone desperately to boost his morale."

"Jack? The professor is as cold as a cucumber and twice as insensitive. He's not going to give up."

"You're wrong, Florence," I said. "Inside, Jack's in a real panic. He hides it well and he's probably rationalized it to something in the nature of philosophical indifference, but I'm telling you the truth. He's our weak sister right now."

She pulled at her earlobe and wrinkled her forehead in thought. Then she said, "You could be right. Nobody can remain that calm and objective with death always so close. I'll make a pitch, Vic. It'll give me something to do."

As I started out Georgia woke up and stretched. She looked at me out of half-opened eyes. "I was dreaming about you. Vic," she said.

"Yeah?" I said.

"You were beating me with a whip…It felt so good!"

I closed the door hard.

CHAPTER TWENTY-SEVEN

WE REORGANIZED OUR WORK SCHEDULES completely on February 26th and began the long labor that would lead us out of our entombment.

Bill Wernecke's hourly readings of the pressure meter and his computations that morning had shown clearly that we would have about 42 days of safety in the Harrow farmhouse, if the rate of glacial movement did not accelerate. But Gabe Harrow warned me when I saw him at noon that we should not rely upon the readings of the pressure gauge for computing ice movement and that so many factors would enter into this—which we could not possibly measure or anticipate—that it was foolhardy to depend upon our meter.

I went to Gabe's room to check on his condition, as I had been doing daily for some time, and I found him propped up in bed reading Constance's *Analysis of Q-Phenomena*.

"Hello, Vic," he said in his listless voice. "Checking on the invalid?"

"When are you going to get out of that bed?"

He closed his eyes for a moment, declining to answer. "How are things going with the group?" he asked.

"We've started to assemble our snowmobile—Steve Engles has taken on that job—and we've got a gang burning out a tunnel to the top of the snow."

"What's the weather data?"

"Wind at eighty-eight miles per hour this morning. Temperature at eleven degrees below zero, about average for this area. The snowfall continues at about twenty inches per day officially. Unofficially it's much more than that."

"Jack Osborne and Rufe Howard both told me of your decision to prepare to move up and away. You've got to wait until the storms level off and particularly for it to warm up at the Equator. If you try to go down there now you'll find it worse than Kansas, and you won't have any Harrow farm to hide out in."

"We've got to anticipate the movement of the ice," I told him. "Our pressure meter shows we've got some forty-two days of safety here. So we'll have no Harrow farm in Kansas either by the end of March."

"Don't bother with that pressure gauge," he said. "I've been giving the matter some thought and I can tell you it's entirely undependable. Glacial movement is controlled by more factors than you could possibly measure from our confined position down under the snow. The meter may read from a few pounds to thousands of pounds per square inch, yet it would not necessarily indicate glacial movement. We can remain at Harrow in safety for at least four months."

I shook my head and backed towards the door. "I have always respected your opinions, Gabe," I said, "but I am not interested in theories of glacial movement. I am interested only in the amount of pressure against our house generated by the ice that surrounds us. This pressure is increasing hourly, as our gauge shows. If the rate of increase is not arrested because of some factor which we cannot now possibly anticipate, then Harrow farmhouse will be crushed in forty-two days."

"I'll not go along with your notions," he said, "or leave Harrow house in forty-two days."

I left him and went through the tunnel to the East Barn where the melting out of the tunnel ramp to the surface had been begun under the direction of Bill Wernecke.

Because we had a wheeled vehicle to take to the surface and because the roadway of our ramp would be ice, we could make the grade no steeper than ten per cent, and even this might tax the traction of our snowmobile wheels to the utmost, for all I knew. However, Wernecke and Steve Engles had anticipated this difficulty of traction and were designing the installation of a thrust engine at the rear of the snowmobile to be operated by the small Kincadium reactor. They were going to use the spare engine from Gabe's Fox-Ring, which had been stored among the materials of the barn. They would have to cut the thrust way down—to the area of 10,000 pounds or so—but Steve assured me this could be done easily with a modification of the reactor output.

The mathematics told us we would build a roadway and tunnel some 3,500 feet long to reach the surface of the snow, which we estimated would be about 600 feet deep by the time we were ready to use our ramp the middle of March. The ramp building was not a simple operation. Provision had to be made first for the tons of water that would cascade down from our snow melting within the tunnel. We would build it by melting the snow with Cory converters, of course. Wernecke and his work gang, which was comprised of Perry Lawrence and his two sons, young Tony Wernecke and Bob Jordan, thawed out the underground drainage system for the barn and found they could keep it open with heat forced through the pipes with blowers. They built a sluiceway out of wood to a drainage opening under the barn, keeping it all heated. The actual ramp building was under way in the afternoon and by dinnertime they had progressed more than 50 feet into the ice.

Dinner that night was a sort of celebration of the beginning of the work to free ourselves, and the only cross words heard all evening were a remark by Georgia Lawrence to Bob Jordan. I tried to get Gabe Harrow to join us but he refused. Florence Donner and Jack Osborne were eating together in a corner of the room and I joined them with Marge.

"We've got to decide fairly soon what we're going to do with Gabe," I told Jack. "We can't let him withdraw this way. He hasn't been in a rational state since the tragic death of Elaine. I concede that the degree is slight, but it is irrationality nevertheless. Gabe rejects the idea that anything will happen to this house—that it will be crushed by the ice movement."

"You must have some logical basis for these so-called facts," Jack said.

"I have the logical basis of my own observation, of Rufe Howard's, and the history of the pressure meter which we installed to measure the ice movement," I replied. "The pressure meter was designed and installed by Bill Wernecke under Gabe's direction, and at that time Gabe declared that when the glacial action started, the meter would register it accurately."

"Changing conditions could have altered his opinion," Jack countered.

"There have been no changed conditions," I said.

Marge put a hand on my arm. "You said you weren't going to argue, Vic. Jack will swing over to our side quickly enough when the house begins to groan and shake."

"So will I," said Florence. "There's no argument like a groaning house."

"I'll go see Gabe," said Jack, smiling thinly at Florence's remark. "I agree that his withdrawal is not a healthy condition."

When he had left, I asked Florence if she was making progress. She shook her head.

"He's a very frightened man," she said. "He's got a shell as thick as a coconut, so the fright doesn't come through very often."

"Well, keep after him," I said. "It isn't his fear I'm worried about. It's his control."

CHAPTER TWENTY-EIGHT

BY THE FIRST WEEK in March our tunnel was progressing at several feet a day. As the tunnel extended upward, more of us had to join the work force to keep the water unfrozen and flowing freely to the drain. It necessitated delicate handling of the converters or we would have ruined our roadway. By the time the tunnel was within fifty feet of the surface, our entire company, with the exception of Steve Engles, Gabe Harrow and Alice Wernecke, were spaced out along its length keeping the ice from clogging it and the water flowing.

On March 16, with our tunnel only feet away from the upper world, the snowmobile assembly was completed and the entire company gathered in the barn to examine it. We had great difficulty persuading Gabe to join us, but he finally consented. It was the first time he had left his room since the New Year.

The vehicle's four wheels were ten feet high and the diameter of each huge tire was four feet. Mounted high up between the wheels was the permanium cabin, twenty-eight feet long, nine feet wide and seven feet high. The interior of the cabin was beautifully appointed with the seats and their arrangement from a ring-transport. The seats were convertible into beds and there was a row of folding bunks on each side above them. The galley was amidships, the controls forward on the port side and there was storage space for several tons of food under the floor. There was a separate communications booth up front on the starboard. Every possible device for survival had been installed, including oxygen generators in the event we should become buried under the snow, and safety belts for rough going. Converter nozzles were so arranged that we could melt our way through the deepest snowdrifts and presumably out of any crevasse we might fall into.

Steve Engles proudly showed off the various installations as though they were his own. Martha Wernecke was ecstatic about the galley and the new electronic cooking oven, which operated on the theta-principle. "It's a crime that we have nothing but concentrates to prepare," she said. "You could do wonders with fresh roasts in this gadget."

The controls, mounted on a panel to the left of the steering wheel, were basic and clearly marked. Steve gave a first lecture on their operation to Bill Wernecke, Bob Jordan and myself.

"The wheels operate independently and each of these four buttons controls the power," he explained. "This bar operates all four at once and the speed is controlled by either this foot pedal or by the bar. The red button cuts off the power and applies the brakes. This group of buttons activates the converters and up here we have the heat and light controls. There's nothing to get out of kilter—unless we let the converters run too high and melt ourselves into a hole."

The main navigating instrument was a Dace Recorder, such as used on space vehicles but modified for our turtle-progress. This instrument recorded time, direction and distance in miles and contained its own gyrocompass, speedometer and chronometer, as well as an automatic calculator. In addition there were independent compass repeaters, speedometers and a Haverwood Navigator. The Dace Recorder would give us our position on its own chart, as well as telling us when we would arrive at any given point. The Haverwood Navigator contained its own miniature Solar System and would give us hourly celestial fixes as well as work out course and distance to any desired point.

Just under the windshield beside the forward compass repeater was a 30-inch Maser Screen which could "see" up to 50 miles ahead. This was the latest development in electronic vision equipment and used infrared and supersonic rays as well as the electronic to describe any obstructions lying within a 180-degree arc. Objects could be focused to within a few feet and could be observed even in color if the operator so desired.

As the group started to leave the vehicle, Gabe came forward and spoke to Steve and myself.

"It's a good machine and it should do its designed job," he said. "Thank you for letting me see it."

"Don't thank us," said Steve. "It's yours as much as anybody's."

Gabe shook his head. Then he looked at me with the defiance of a small boy. "I'm going to stay here with Elaine."

"Let's walk back to the house," I said.

I took Gabe back to his room and I talked to him of incidents in the past when he and Elaine and I were together. He seemed to enjoy my reminiscences and he became quite animated. I realized then that his mind had retired entirely from reality.

On the evening of that day, March 16th, I got an urgent summons from Florence to come to the communications room. She had a speaker on the UHF turned up loud and a man's voice was reporting incidents that were happening about him. There was terror and panic in his voice.

"...now shaking as though we were in an earthquake," he said. "There is a loud rumble underneath that sounds like thunder. The entire staff has lit out for the lower floors... There it goes again! My God, we are falling! We are falling over! My God! My God!"

His voice suddenly went off the air. Florence clicked off the receiver.

"That was the end of the Chicago Complex Weather Bureau," she said. "They've just gone off the air for good."

"The Corning Tower!" I exclaimed. "It's collapsed!"

She nodded. "You should have heard the first part of it. The reports were coming up to the station from the people down below. The ice had started to move and they knew their building was going to cave in on them. This man on the air was reporting everything they said. It was the most tragic thing I've ever heard."

Jack Osborne came into the room and Florence told him what had just happened. He listened to her dramatic account with a look of horror on his face, then he sat down slowly at the table and ran his fingers through his sparse hair.

"The point is," said Florence, "that we're all terrified—all of us who are alive. I'm terrified and Vic is terrified and Gabe and the Jordans and the Lawrences. But we're going to try to save ourselves just the same."

"I can't take it as well as the rest of you," Jack said in a low voice.

"You're taking it as well as anyone could expect," I told him.

Later on that evening Bill Wernecke showed me the latest computations for his readings of the pressure meter. The meter had shown a pressure reading of 1,200 pounds per square inch on March 7th, after having risen slowly and steadily to that point. Then it had leveled off for eight days, gaining only a few pounds in that period.

Bill had been frank to say he couldn't account for the leveling off and he had been inclined to adopt Gabe Harrow's view that the meter was not dependable and that we might have another four months of safety in the farmhouse. We had discussed this at length on the previous night (March 15th) and had finally agreed to wait another week before making any decision.

Now on the night of March 16th the meter had suddenly gone crazy. The pressure was up by 500 pounds in the 24-hour period and seemed to be rising fast.

"I would say," he warned, "that a definite ice movement is under way, and our situation will become critical in a matter of hours."

"Get everyone in the living room including Gabe Harrow," I told him. "Sound the general alarm."

Gabe was the first to greet me, standing by the hallway entrance with Bill Wernecke. Bill was holding his arm with what might have been restraint.

Gabe demanded, "What right have you to order the invasion of my privacy?"

"We're moving out, Gabe," I told him gently. "The ice has started to move and your house will be unsafe in a matter of hours."

"Poppycock!" he exclaimed.

He attempted to jerk away from Bill but he was unable to. He stood glaring at me like a small boy.

I turned to the others, standing beside Gabe in the doorway. I said, "There is definite evidence that glacial movement has started and that we must leave Harrow farm immediately. We have ample time to gather our belongings and to load the snowmobile. None of you should feel apprehensive or allow yourselves to become panicked by anything that may happen or may be said. Our situation is not dangerous at this hour and there is no reason to be moved by any unusual fears... This is what we have been waiting for these many miserable months—to get out and away."

I read off the work assignments I had prepared and told them all to get cracking. A cheer went up when I had finished.

CHAPTER TWENTY-NINE

ON MARCH 17TH at 3:47 A.M. the Harrow Group left Harrow farm in Fallon, Kansas.

Four hours of hard work by all of us had preceded this moment. The snowmobile had been loaded completely. We had stowed all but a few pounds of our food and the rest of the storage space had been packed with the necessities— mostly our tools.

Each member of the group was permitted two suits of heated Fincham arctics, two pairs of heated snow boots, one helmet, two pairs of gloves and a dressing gown. Towels, linens, and toilet articles were in ample supply. We took along a dozen packs of cards and score pads for Bridge and a few boards for more modern games. However, we didn't anticipate much game playing.

The loading had been done by Bob and Libby Jordan and the Lawrences, including Georgia, under the direction of Steve Engles. He had adopted the snowmobile in a very personal way and he seemed to consider it his own property. None of us disputed him since he had assembled it, with some help from Jack Osborne, and he certainly knew more about its operation and potentials than any of us. The final installation on our vehicle, made in the last two hours, had been the thrust engine and Bill Wernecke had done that alone. It had been a simple matter of welding brackets to the frame at the rear and mounting the engine and reactor.

Then, with the loading completed and all on board our vehicle with the exception of Gabe Harrow, who had barricaded himself in his room as the work started, Rufe Howard and I went back to the farmhouse.

The house was creaking and shuddering and total collapse could not have been more than half an hour away.

I forced my way into Gabe's room with Rufe Howard behind me and I faced an angry Gabe with an old-fashioned electronic pistol in his hand.

"Stand where you are or I'll fire!" he yelled.

I stood. I said, "The house is about ready to go, Gabe. You coming with us?"

"No, damn it, no!" he exclaimed. "I'm not going to leave Elaine!"

"Will you let Rufe leave some medicine with you before he goes?" I asked him.

"I don't need any medicine!"

"I have these for you," said Rufe, stepping toward him and offering some ampoules in his hand. "You'll need them in case you get hurt. Relieve the pain."

Gabe looked at him suspiciously but lowered his gun. "What are they?" he asked.

"Acatin sulfide," said Rufe. "Absolutely harmless. I can give you a shot now and you'll see. All the pain goes and you're in a world all of your own."

Gabe sat on the bed and put his head in his hands. He had dropped his pistol on the floor and I picked it up. He said, "I'll try one, Rufe. I feel like hell."

Rufe Howard took a syringe from a case, broke off the head of an ampoule and filled it. He unbuttoned Gabe's shirt and plunged the needle gently into his right shoulder. Then he stood back and nodded at me.

I picked Gabe up and carried him out of the house and through the tunnel to the snowmobile. Steve Engles took him from me and lifted him inside. Rufe Howard followed him in. I took a last look around as I started up the ladder. All the lights had been left on and I could see a small part of the porch at the end of our tunnel. The creaking of the house had grown louder and could be heard clearly. There was also a rumbling as of far-off thunder.

I latched the snowmobile door and told Steve, "Let's get going."

BOOK TWO

Escape

CHAPTER ONE

ON MARCH 17TH, 2204, the temperature was ten degrees below zero, the wind was from the West at 75 miles per hour with gusts up to 90; the snow was falling at about a half an inch per hour and visibility was ten feet. That was the difference. We hadn't been able to report visibility since September.

Our snowmobile had negotiated the tunnel and ramp from Harrow farm in six minutes, and suddenly we were out on top of a violent night with the snow swirling around us and the gale roaring at us and shaking our vehicle as though some giant hand had seized it. Steve pulled the switch shutting off the thrust engine and said, "Course zero nine eight. All four wheels ahead slow. What orders, Captain?"

I was sitting just behind him at the navigator's desk, looking at the faces of our company in the lighted cabin. Gabe and Rufe Howard were in the first seat to my left, just behind the communications booth. Gabe was asleep and Rufe was looking ahead with intense concentration as though he were trying to pierce the snow blanket. Behind them sat Georgia alone, her legs across the seat and her head resting on the padding around the window. She was looking without expression at the cabin roof, but her face seemed white and drawn. Across from Georgia were Marge and Alice Wernecke. Alice was sitting straight and composed and Marge was smiling at her. Marge looked up and caught my eye. She pointed upward and shivered as a gust of wind grabbed and shook us. Behind Marge were Florence Donner and Jack Osborne. Florence was talking to him and he was listening intently. Across from them were Libby and Bob

Jordan, holding each other's hands, tense looks on their faces. Behind the Jordans were Bill and Martha Wernecke. Martha looked upset and Bill appeared to be reassuring her. Perry and Sylvia Lawrence and their two boys and Tony Wernecke were in the rear seats behind the galley. All of them were looking about, apparently listening to the gale.

"Steady as you go," I told Steve. "Take it easy while we test the holding power of this snow. Keep it around two knots."

"I would judge the wheels are sinking only a few feet below the crust," Steve said. "Traction is excellent." We talked to each other through the intercom, the roar of the gale was so loud.

Bill Wernecke came forward to watch the operation and familiarize himself with the controls. Bill and Bob Jordan had been designated as relief pilots and would take over for four-hour periods. I had worked out a very loose schedule of assignments for the company. Most of the restrictions and regimentation of our under-snow confinement had been abandoned as unnecessary now that we were traveling. The constant wind and snow were bound to become irritating and in time bring us to new depressions, but meanwhile it was better, I believed, for all of us to do as we pleased and enjoy what freedom was available in our cramped machine.

As we moved ahead, I became aware of an insistent cater-wauling, barely audible over the roar of the gale. Our radio receivers, which I had forgotten completely. I crossed to the communications booth and turned the dials on both the VHF and UHF. The air was full of music, voice and code broadcasts. It seemed the whole world was alive and sending its sounds through the air as in the old days before our en-tombment.

I motioned to Florence Donner to join me. She was amazed by the air activity and turned the VHF dial to the lower ranges. A flood of music suddenly filled the booth.

"That's Missouri Center!" she exclaimed. "There's one thing for sure, the world isn't dead yet."

"You monitor the broadcasts and find out what stations are on the air in this vicinity," I told her. "Also make a list of everything you can bring in between here and Norfolk Complex."

I went back to the control station and dimmed the lights in the cabin. We were confined to a gale-tossed world of solid white and it was impossible to tell where the snowfall ended and the surface began. All we could see was the white gale that closed in on us almost as though we were in the center of a snowdrift. Our lights only accentuated the whiteness and we finally dimmed our headlights to minimum to avoid the glare. We were using the modern arcanium vapor lamps which are supposed to penetrate mist and fog. They were useless.

Bill Wernecke was in the co-pilot's seat and handling the snowmobile controls when a half hour away from Harrow farm we ran head on into an area of snow so soft it would not sustain our weight. We couldn't go over it so we stopped dead in our tracks, the snow packed hard under us and the wheels spinning uselessly.

There was a moment of panic in the cabin as the cessation of forward motion and the vibration of the free-spinning wheels communicated themselves to the company. I grabbed the mike of the intercom hanging overhead and spoke authoritatively. "Keep your places. We have merely encountered a soft area. There is no emergency."

Georgia said over the communications booth mike, "There's no emergency except that we're stuck."

That brought general laughter, and much banter followed over the intercom.

Steve took over the controls and turned on the forward and undercarriage converters. We were free almost instantly and he moved the machine ahead slow. We had gone forward about ten feet when it became apparent that we were headed down a steep incline. Just as Steve brought the snowmobile to a halt the sides of our trench caved in on us and the moving, swirling world around us was blanked out.

There were several loud cries of dismay that could be heard over the muffled growl of the storm.

Steve turned on all converters and we started to back out of the declivity. We were clear of it in five minutes and back on the relatively solid crust.

"We go around this place," I told Steve. "Bear to the right for a few minutes. I'll call the courses. Steer one eight five now."

We proceeded on that heading for a hundred yards, then turned east again and suddenly we were plunging once more into the soft area. I had ordered all of our company to fasten their safety belts and there was less dismay and confusion from our second sortie into the declivity. We backed out immediately with the aid of our converters and continued on south to find a way around this area. We found a supporting crust extending east within three miles and we were beginning to relax and establish a routine for steady travel when we came suddenly into a second area of soft snow like the first. We handled this occasion with much more efficiency and within minutes we were on a course north seeking to find more solid crust that extended east.

Within a couple of hours most of our company had made up their bunks and were fast asleep. They had stopped worrying at least that much about our slow progress and the uncertain snow crust.

CHAPTER TWO

OUR FIRST DAWN in almost six months was a miserably dirty gray that added nothing to the outlook of our prospects. It did give us a few feet more of visibility, however, so it was welcomed extravagantly by Steve, Bill, and myself, who had remained at our several posts more out of curiosity about our machine than any dedication to duty.

We maintained a speed of about four knots, which we found to be the maximum for safety. At 7:00 A.M. I turned over the navigation to Rufe Howard (he was an old sailboat man and could read the charts) and Bob Jordan took the controls. I crawled into a bunk next to Marge.

At 11:05 Bill Wernecke shook me awake and handed me a cup of steaming coffee. "We're over Missouri Center," he said. "Rufe wanted me to tell you."

I drank the coffee and then joined Rufe, Bob Jordan and Steve at the front end.

"The Murphy Brain says we're right over Lopatka Square," said Rufe. "There's nothing much showing on the Maser Screen except a big drift off to the left. That would be along the river bank."

"No buildings?" I asked.

He shook his head. "Nothing. The Board of Trade should be just off to the left. The Maser Screen is blank in that whole area."

Marge had come up to the front end and was standing just behind me. "I wonder how many are alive?" she said.

"You can't tell what happened down there," said Rufe. "There could be a sizeable community down below living the life we lived back at Harrow farm."

Bob Jordan had stopped the snowmobile while we talked and several more of our company came forward.

Martha Wernecke, who had heard Rufe's speculation, said, "Maybe we should go down there. We could give them hope. If they could just see us then they would know there are others struggling to save themselves. We could show them our machine and tell them our plans. Maybe they could build one like it and follow us."

"That's unlikely," said Bob Jordan. "However, I am certainly not opposed to helping my fellow man, even to the minimum of giving him hope."

"Then we must go down," exclaimed Marge.

Gabe Harrow, who had now fully recovered from Rufe's injection, came to the forward seat on the left and sat listening.

I said, "I am not opposed to going down below the snow if it is feasible...I do not propose to risk our safety, however. We cannot melt our way from the top of the snow to the bottom with converters because there is no place for the water to run off. It is not at all the same as the tunnel we built upward at Harrow farm. We must find a building standing that rises above the snow and descend inside it. If we cannot find such a building, then we will not go below."

"Let's hunt for a building then," said Bill Wernecke. "Vic's proposal makes sense to me."

"Is that the general consensus?" I asked.

The affirmatives seemed to be unanimous. Then Gabe Harrow spoke up.

"Let these people be in peace," he said. "You can share nothing with them but our own hopelessness."

"That's a lot of nonsense!" exclaimed Bill Wernecke. "We've been doing damned well from day to day. You've given up, Gabe. That's your trouble."

Gabe sank down in his seat. "Why shouldn't I give up?" he mumbled.

Jack Osborne moved to his side and put a hand on his shoulder. "Look, Gabe, we're all scared," he said. "I've just begun to realize that my fear is a normal state and nothing to be ashamed of. Come back to us, my friend, and stand by our sides. We need you."

Florence Donner, standing just behind Jack, was looking at him proudly. Gabe shook his head slowly and passed a shaking hand over his forehead. "Yes, I am afraid," he said.

"Now we're getting somewhere!" said Rufe Howard in a hearty voice. "When you've admitted that you've admitted everything."

Gabe smiled up at him wanly. He got to his feet and looked around at us, then over at Bob Jordan in the pilot's seat.

"Come on over and learn how to run this contraption," Bob told him.

He shook his head and walked back to the stem.

We started out from Lopatka Square, Missouri Center, to hunt for a building that was still standing above the snow. Our Maser Screen revealed no such structure, but the screen showed several smaller drifts ahead over the center of the city and it was my notion that one of them might be hiding a building. I gave Bob Jordan the course for the nearest, and we started out.

We reached the first drift and nudged into it, our forward converters going. We had melted the snow halfway through and had started to sink into a soft spot before we gave up on it and backed out.

The second drift hid nothing but more snow. The third one we tried brought us to the top floors of the old Lemmon Tower at Wingate Road.

I organized a survey party of Bill Wernecke, the three Lawrences, Perry, Fred and Sam Houston, and myself. We equipped ourselves with Bandburger torches, a Cory converter, a compass and an FX-phone to keep in touch with the snowmobile.

The windows of the Lemmon Tower were of permanium and we had to burn one of them through with the converter to gain access. We entered into the long-abandoned office of a law firm. There was mold over everything, and the smell of decay. We went out into the main hallway and passed the bank of silent elevators on our way to the enclosed stairway.

We started down the forty flights to the bottom, stopping on each floor to make certain it was uninhabited.

We encountered no human being all the way to the bottom—only rats. We saw hundreds scurrying along the halls and down the stairway ahead of us. They didn't look or act particularly hungry. As we got lower, there was the definite odor of death.

The building was fairly warm—about 35 degrees—and there was slight warmth coming from the vents that we passed. Apparently the reactor was still operating, although it did not give out enough energy to activate the lights. None of the switches worked. I tried a phone in one of the offices and got only a blank screen with no glow at all.

On the main floor, a huge marble lobby two stories high furnished with leather chairs and divans, we were met with a sight of horror. Nearly two hundred dead were crowded into this huge room, in the chairs and divans and on the floor, men, women and children, their bodies in advanced stages of decay. The airtight fire doors had kept most of the stench from the stairway, so we were unprepared for what we found.

The only way out was through the lobby and we took no deep breaths until we were outside the building. At the front a tunnel through the ice about five feet wide and six high appeared to have been recently dug out. I led the way into it, carrying torch and converter. We walked about a thousand feet west and the tunnel turned sharply south and nearly doubled in size. There were lights on poles along one side. Three hundred feet further along we came to the lighted entrance to a modern building I thought I recognized. I looked for the plaque on the side where I had remembered it. The plaque read *Mid-Continent Oil Trust,* as it should have.

We five stopped and looked at the building entrance with amazement. The steps were immaculate and the permanium doors polished. We could see through the doors to the inside and people seemed to be moving about in a normal way.

We went in and stood near the door watching the activity.

A well-dressed woman of middle age detached herself from a group near a desk and came over to us. She greeted us warmly, saying, "Welcome to our refuge, strangers. Will you please come with me and I will have you meet our director?"

I motioned to my group to follow. We were escorted to an office in a corner and presented to the director as "five more refugees." His name was Cranston Whitford and he acted the part of a most gracious host.

"I am Colonel Victor Savage," I said, shaking hands with him, "and we are all members of the Harrow Group. Dr. Gabriel Harrow and the rest of our company are up on top of the snow waiting for us."

"Well, now!" he exclaimed, "our first snow travelers! I can hardly believe it! How did you get down to us?"

"Through the Lemmon Tower," I said.

"Oh, dear, that dreadful place!" he said. "All those poor people. They had refused to join us, you know. Said the snow would be over in a few days. By the time we got the tunnel to them, they were all dead. Now tell me, Colonel, what can we do for you? Food, reactor fuel, shelter? You name it and it's yours."

I laughed. "You've turned the tables on us," I said. "We came down to help you!"

"Oh no! That's very funny!" He laughed shortly, then his face got serious. "And very gallant of you, also. No, my friend, we are all well fixed at the bottom of the snow until the storm stops, unless something untoward happens."

"Something untoward will happen long before then," I told him. "Glacial movement of the ice has already started in many areas. We left Fallon, Kansas, just before our house was destroyed by ice movement. On the same day the Corning Tower in Chicago was crushed."

"Yes, very unfortunate. It was on the UHF. Well, we don't go along with your pessimism, Colonel. The snow will stop shortly and the ice will melt and that will be an end to it."

"Do you want to hear the views of Dr. Gabriel Harrow and Professor Jack Wheeler Osborne and Dr. Robert Crist Jordan of our group about these matters?" I asked him.

"Bless you, no!" he exclaimed, smiling broadly. "I have nothing against these men personally, Colonel. In fact, I admire them for their sincerity, whether or not it is misplaced. No, we are well advised, Colonel, and we do not wish to hear more of the pessimistic outlook. Professor Duncan Curran and Dr. Alexis Vidal are both with us here on our Board, and we feel that their knowledge is sufficient to guide us."

"It has been a great pleasure to meet you," I said, extending my hand. "I regret deeply that you will not listen to us."

"You will see," he said. "The snow will end within another thirty days and the ice will begin to melt. Come back again, Colonel, you and your friends. You shall always be welcome here."

"I'm afraid not," I said as we left.

CHAPTER THREE

IF THERE IS any single thing that brought Gabe Harrow back to us and to the world of the living, I would judge it to be the report I gave to the company from Missouri Center and Mr. Cranston Whitford.

"Why, damn those nitwits!" Gabe exploded finally. "Do they still refuse to believe what is happening to them and the world?"

"Apparently they repose their confidence in Curran and Vidal," I said. "Both of them are in Missouri Center and are members of their board of directors."

Gabe shook his head in perplexity. "I can't understand those two," he said. "Why should they mislead these people with false predictions?"

"Perhaps the predictions are not false," I said. "Perhaps the storms will end within thirty days." I didn't believe that at all, but it seemed to me Gabe's anger was the most hopeful sign I'd seen since the New Year.

"What!" he demanded. "You, too!"

I nodded at him. "I won't actually know until thirty days have elapsed whether the prediction is true or false."

"You know!" he said scornfully. Then he laughed suddenly. "I think all of you are trying to badger me. It serves me right."

"I've told you the truth, Gabe," I said. "At least about the Missouri Center survivors. They are satisfied in their ignorance and there was nothing we could have said to make them aware of their peril."

"Then we will go somewhere else where people will listen to sense!" he exclaimed.

"You name it," I said. "So long as it's east of here, we can go."

"I must convince people of the truth!" he said.

"All you can hope to do is to convince them that they will die sooner than they think."

"They can build vehicles and get out, just as we are doing!"

He was angry again and he had lost completely the apathy that had held him for so long.

"Come on up and learn how to run this machine," I told him. "You can pilot us to your mountain where you will deliver your sermon."

CHAPTER FOUR

IN THE CENTER of Missouri province, which corresponds roughly to the former State of the same name, there lies the Dome City of Franklin, which was one of the first of the covered communities designed to counteract radiation resulting from the World Wars. It may be interesting to note here that the Franklin Dome was the first ever to be constructed of permanium and that in those early days, before the development of the Cory converter, there was no known method of breaching this material short of blasting it with a fusion bomb.

Bill Wernecke started a discussion of Franklin as we left the vicinity of Lemmon Tower in Missouri City, with Gabe at the snowmobile controls.

"That permanium dome of theirs just might have held up under this snow," said Bill. "Permanium is supposed to have fantastic tensile strength under controlled temperature conditions, but what would happen to it in cold weather under the enormous weight of the snow, I would have no idea. If this dome has held up, then we might find an entire city that has survived, and with few hardships."

"I would doubt the picture is so optimistic," said Gabe. "I've never heard anything good about permanium except for glazing windows."

"I don't think we'll find conditions there very good," said Florence Donner. "Their VM and VK stations went off the air very early, and since last night I've been able to raise only one VHF station broadcasting from Franklin. It is a code station, apparently Government, and was asking for weather reports. If there are many still alive down there, they're not very well organized for communications."

"Try to raise them on our own broadcasting set," I told her, "and see if you can get a report on conditions."

I went back to the rear where Steve was sitting in earnest conversation with Georgia Lawrence. As I approached I could hear the tones of a quarrel. Georgia stopped talking when she saw me coming and leaned back in her seat in what might have been a languorous manner.

"Weren't you in Franklin at the Navy Reactor School?" I asked Steve.

"Yes, for a couple of years after I got out of the Academy," he replied.

"What about this Franklin Dome? Seems to me I heard they opened up the top of it for ventilation."

"They did, back in eighty-seven," he said. "They installed half a dozen blowers around the top. The openings were about fifty feet across. It turned out to be a bad idea, though, because it lowered the air pressure and made all of the oxygen generators work overtime. They turned off the blowers a couple of years later."

"We'd have to keep off the top of the dome or we might go through a hole," I said.

"That's a thought," he replied. "I wouldn't suppose the top of the dome would be safe unless the snow were awfully deep. But on the other hand, I wouldn't think the dome could support too much snow with those holes in it. They would certainly destroy the strength of the arch."

I started back forward and Steve got up to follow me. Georgia called to him, "Hey, where are you going?"

"I'll be back in a minute," he told her.

"Don't bother," she said. "I've been bored enough by you for one day."

When we got up to the control station, Steve said to me, "It's all I can do sometimes to keep from strangling her."

Gabe, Steve, Bob Jordan and I discussed our approach to Franklin, 95 miles east of Missouri Center.

"If the dome hasn't collapsed, we'll have to keep off the top of it," I said. "Steve informs me there are six openings in the top fifty feet in diameter."

"If the dome has collapsed we'll never get down to Franklin," said Bob Jordan. "As you pointed out back at M.C., we can't melt our way down. There's no place for the water to run off."

"I've been thinking about that," I replied. "They've got a VHF station operating there. We can talk to them when we get over the city and ask them to melt out a ramp up to us, as we did back at Harrow farm. They'd surely have a couple of Cory converters down there."

"Not necessarily," said Steve. "A lot of city governments don't like these converters and they've been outlawed most everywhere outside of backward Kansas."

Florence came out of the communications cabin then, her face flushed with anger.

"Franklin won't talk to us," she said. "Some officious so-and-so told me to get off the air, that their channel had been reserved for emergency use only, and that I was violating the law."

"Tell him to go to hell," I said.

"Oh, I did that," she replied.

CHAPTER FIVE

ON MARCH 18TH shortly before midnight there was a noticeable increase in wind velocity and our snowmobile shook and plunged like a boat in a hurricane. We estimated that the gale was well over 100 miles per hour.

I took a tour down along the aisle and checked on our company. Georgia was in the communications cabin, her face tense. She managed a wink at me nevertheless. Marge was lying in the upper bunk just aft of the cabin and she stared at me out of dull, pained eyes when I parted the curtains.

"I'm sick, darling," she said. "Please forgive me but I—I feel terribly nauseated."

"You're seasick," I said. "All you want to do is die… Now seasickness comes from being frightened. This is an awfully silly contraption to be out in on a night like this."

"Thanks for your reassuring words," she said. "How can you go around looking so damned confident all the time?"

"I'm not confident. I'll give you ten to one right now that I'll go into hysterics before the night is over."

"Phooey! Go away."

I talked to Bob and Libby Jordan and Martha Wernecke for a time, mostly about the wind and the exaggerated motion of our vehicle. Bob and Martha said they were getting used to it. Libby opined that she never would.

Sylvia and Perry Lawrence and the two boys were all asleep in stern bunks, as were the Wernecke children. Steve Engles, Rufe Howard, Gabe Harrow and Jack Osborne were sitting at the small galley table trying to keep cups of coffee from spilling over.

"How do you account for this sudden increase in the wind, Gabe?" I asked.

"It's not a sudden increase," he replied. "It's all relative— the wind's going to blow anywhere from sixty to a hundred and fifty miles an hour until we get to the leveling-off stage, and that shouldn't come until the Fall Equinox. No one can tell now what the weather's going to be from day to day, except that it's going to be bad."

"Not even Vidal or Curran?" I asked him.

He snorted. "Those two must have found a crystal ball. What are they basing their observations on, a barometer? Air pressure hasn't meant anything since September, except in the upper strata, and they're not getting any reports from up there any more than I am."

"They can still contact the Plymouth Platforms," I said.

"They're too far out," he said. "You know what the Platforms are reporting right now? That it's snowing on Earth. Well we know that."

CHAPTER SIX

ON MARCH 20TH at 8:31 A.M. we suffered our first major accident. Our snowmobile, piloted by Bob Jordan, encountered an unusually sudden and steep area of soft snow and sank by the bow before it could be brought to an emergency stop. Bob turned on the undercarriage converters immediately and melted the snow holding our chassis. As he started to back out, our vehicle tipped to the right at an angle of about 40 degrees, so for a moment it was off balance in two directions, the front end tipping down and the whole machine leaning to the right. At that moment a vicious gust of wind hit us like a sledgehammer and over we went on our right side, slamming into the snow with a thud. The gust must have had 150 miles an hour of violence behind it.

Many of us were shaken and bruised, even with our safety belts and the complete padding of the interior. The two Wernecke children were both yelling, but Alice quieted immediately when Martha spoke to her. Others were moaning and all were exclaiming their dismay. I got on the intercom immediately—I had been dozing in the navigator's seat—and called for a work party of the three Lawrences.

"Put on arctics, hoods and snow boots," I ordered. "Break out the converter in the center hatch...I will lead the way out."

I told Steve Engles to take the controls and I took one of the Corning jacks and a second converter from their brackets at the front end. I opened the forward roof-hatch with Perry Lawrence's help. I melted the snow away from the hatch and climbed out with the converter and jack. I slid down in snow and slush almost up to my neck.

The others of the work party followed me out and we worked our way around the front of our reclining vehicle to crouch beside one of the huge front wheels. The wind was as bad as it possibly could have been. The snow swirled at us like a solid wall and it was impossible to stand up against it and the hurricane behind it. Perry turned his converter on me to melt the ice forming from the slush I had slid into.

I started melting the snow under the lower front wheel and Perry and Sam Houston used their converter to melt out the rear wheel. The snowmobile suddenly slid down into the holes we had made, partly righting itself to an angle of about 60 degrees.

Fred and I had to scramble away fast to keep from being caught underneath, and I hoped Perry and Sam Houston had been at least as agile. Fred and I crawled up to the rear to check on them and we found that Perry had been conked on the head by a reactor casing. Blood had seeped through his helmet and frozen, and I ordered Sam Houston and Fred to get their father back into the cabin.

I took a converter and the jack around to the other side, moving a couple of inches a minute. I melted a hole in the snow under the side of the cabin about amidships and then waited for the water and slush to freeze. When it was solid, I used this ice for a base and rigged the jack so that it would push the machine upright. Fred and Sam Houston rejoined me just as I got it rigged. We turned on the power on the jack and the snowmobile slowly came to a normal position.

We crawled to the front door, unfroze it with the converter, and climbed back inside.

Steve Engles got the snowmobile back on the crust without further mishap and we were on our way again. Rufe Howard, with Marge acting as aide, was treating the injured. Perry Lawrence was the most seriously hurt. His scalp had been laid open for several inches and Rufe reported he undoubtedly had suffered a concussion. He was put to bed in a stern bunk and ordered to stay there. Tony Wernecke had badly wrenched his shoulder and it was being treated with heat. Martha Wernecke had bit her lower lip painfully and had several bruises on her body, as did Georgia and Jack Osborne.

We arrived in the close vicinity of Franklin seven hours beyond our ETA and I went into the radio cabin with Florence to try to talk to the survivors below and find out whether we could get down to them.

I tuned into the Franklin wavelength and heard nothing. I started calling their station by voice and after five minutes I received a reply.

"This is Franklin communications central," a man's voice said. "Kindly state your business."

"Harrow Group calling," I replied. "We are in the vicinity of your city on top of the snow. We desire to assist you in any way possible. Also we have information vital for your safety and survival."

"Don't be insolent," said the voice. "This channel is reserved for official use only. Aren't you the people who cut in on our broadcast four days ago?"

"Affirmative," I said. "Let me speak to somebody in authority."

"I have all the authority necessary," was the reply. "I order you to get off this channel."

"You get somebody immediately," I blasted at him, "or I'll jam your channel down your throat!"

The air went dead and I figured I'd lost that round. But I kept the wavelength tuned in.

Within five minutes the Franklin station came back to life. A suave-voiced gent gave the call letters and inquired for the Harrow Group.

"This is the Harrow Group," I said. "Colonel Savage speaking."

"This is Commissioner Logan," said the voice. "Our communications officials inform me that you consider this to be an emergency."

"Isn't it?" I inquired weakly.

"There is no emergency in Franklin, if that's what you mean to imply," he said. "I was told you wanted to offer assistance. We are assured the storms will be over shortly and we are well able to take care of ourselves until then."

"The storms will *not* be over shortly," I said. I couldn't keep the exasperation out of my voice. "Will you please speak to Dr. Gabriel Harrow, who is with us here?"

I called Gabe into the booth. "Tell Commissioner Logan what the score is," I said, handing him the microphone.

Gabe spoke to him for five minutes, telling him of the conditions that would prevail in these latitudes for the next 122 years. He described our vehicle and urged the Commissioner to follow our example and prepare to flee south. When he had finished talking the air was dead for a couple of minutes. Then the Commissioner's voice came on.

"That is very disquieting information," he said. "I took the liberty of having several of my associates listen to you, Dr. Harrow. Now I must ask you please to clear this channel."

"You—you want me to get off the air?" demanded Gabe incredulously.

"If you please, Dr. Harrow," said the Commissioner.

"And you don't want our help or advice?"

"We appreciate your motives, believe me, Dr. Harrow. When the storms end I shall make it a point to report your gallant offer to the Council."

Gabe put the microphone down on the desk and shook his head at Florence.

I picked up the mike. "This is Colonel Savage," I said.

"Will you please tell me, Commissioner, whether the permanium dome has remained intact?"

"I'm sorry," he replied. "That is classified information. Now I must ask you to get off this channel."

Gabe crossed the aisle and slumped into the co-pilot's seat. Rufe Howard, acting as navigator, asked him, "This prophet business getting you down, Gabe?"

CHAPTER SEVEN

WE STAYED over Franklin several hours exploring and listening on all wavelengths for sounds of the life below. We were convinced that the permanium dome had collapsed, otherwise there would have been no point in the information about it being denied to us. We picked up enough interference down in the lower wavelengths to indicate that some 200 reactors were functioning. We picked up one AM broadcast of music, very faintly heard, on the northern perimeter of the city, which was either a closed-circuit system or a theatre.

What it all added up to was a disaster of great scope for Franklin. The collapse of the permanium dome would have been sufficient to wipe out the entire population under it, except for a few fortunate ones far enough underground or in some sections of the perimeter.

"I can't understand why they're so damned secretive," said Gabe. "What have they got to hide? Or do they feel that they are being brave by not telling their troubles to the rest of the world?"

"You can't expect people to act rationally under these conditions," said Jack Osborne. "Those few hundred down there are all in shock. They're going to stay down there and die with the rest of the city."

Gabe looked at him sharply. "I guess that's the way I was back in Fallon," he said. "I think I know how they feel..."

I gave the order to proceed east to Steve Engles, who had taken the controls again. I gave him a course for St. Louis Complex (zero nine two) and I got an ETA from the Murphy Brain of 120 hours for the 135 miles. I had a lot more data to give the computer after our various experiences of detours and the accident on the previous leg, so I judged the time estimate would prove much more accurate.

But the time estimate didn't prove accurate at all. Outside of Franklin we ran into a vast area of soft snow that would not support our vehicle. We first tried to skirt it in a southerly direction and found that the edge of the soft area swung further and further west. Then Bob Jordan foolishly decided to probe the bottom of it to see if we could possibly go through it with our converters and we wound up buried in seventy feet of snow.

It was touch and go to get out. We could use our converters only sparingly or we would have sunk down another 70 feet. It appeared we could move in no direction but downward. The only advantage in our position was that we were out of the storm and the howling wind for the first time since we had left Harrow farm. That was a blessed relief and we all found ourselves suddenly relaxed and talking in normal voices, instead of trying to out shout the gale.

"We've got enough power here to blast us out of the Earth's orbit," said Bill Wernecke, "but what good does it do us? Like our forefathers, we've discovered the limitations of the wheel."

"Wait a minute," I said, "you've given me an idea. Let's turn our buggy around and I'll show you how to get out."

Turning the snowmobile so that it faced back up toward the crust was a long and arduous maneuver and sank us another twenty feet down. Gabe and Steve were at the controls and the rest of us spaced ourselves along the cabin to give the machine balance. When finally we were faced in the right direction I told Steve, "Give all four wheels half power ahead. Douse all converters. Now fire the thrust engine, full power."

We started moving up immediately and in two minutes we were back on the crust—and back into the violence of the storm.

We turned north from that point and didn't reach the limits of the soft area for ten hours. We probed eastward continually, of course, to determine the extent of the soft area, and so our average progress east was not much more than a mile an hour.

The ten-day trip to St. Louis Complex proved to be the furnace that put the final temper on our dispositions. The constant wind, the almost-solid wall of snow, the plunging and yawing of our snowmobile, the utter impossibility of a single moment's relaxation, left our nerves so raw that self-control was supported by the thinnest of threads. By the time we had stopped over the caverns of St. Louis Complex, we of the Harrow group had attained a homogenous entity, aneled by the searing, burning cold, and we would never again cry out in dismay at the unbearable pain that our close presence gave to each other.

There were two tragic exceptions—Georgia Lawrence and Steve Engles.

CHAPTER EIGHT

I CANNOT TELL YOU the full story of Georgia Lawrence and Steve Engles, because the only part of it I saw and heard and know about is a very small fraction of the whole. I have no remote idea how they felt deep inside themselves and what forces impelled them to the final climax of their relationship. I will tell you all I know, but you must supply the motives yourself. I have thought much about these motives but they continue to elude me.

The strain on their relationship seemed to be multiplied enormously by the confinement of the snowmobile. They were together often, sitting side by side in one of the seats, but never during this time did any of us hear them exchange any words of intimacy or even regard. On the contrary, they quarreled continuously, although there was never any real passion behind their deprecatory exchanges. Georgia's remarks seemed to have more edge, to be more bitter than Steve's, but they never raised their voices or in any other way showed deep feeling.

How did they feel about each other, then? Did they love or hate each other? Or were they indifferent, merely rasping each other with barbed words because of their fundamental male-female conflict?

On the eighth day of this miserable period Rufe Howard came to me in the rear of our vehicle where I was dozing in an upper bunk and stood with his head inside the curtains, his mouth close to my ear.

"Have you been noticing Steve?" he asked.

"No," I said. "Not any more than usual."

"He's too calm," said Rufe. "Too controlled."

"Thank God for that. This would be a hell of a time for him to throw a wingding."

"You're not listening," said Rufe. "I said he was *too* controlled. If he'd only lash out, show some emotion, I'd feel a lot better about him. He scares me, this way."

"I'll keep my eye on him," I said, yawning.

"Look, Commander, this is serious. I wouldn't bother you with it if it wasn't. I was just watching Steve and Georgia sitting up behind the radio cabin. She was using vile language—the worst I've ever heard from a woman. Steve had a sort of half smile on his mouth and he was nodding at her as though he agreed with everything she was saying. I can only guess what was going on inside of him. His eyes were almost opaque and hid his feelings well, but they were not the eyes of a normal, rational person, Vic. I had the sudden feeling that at any moment his brain would explode into awful violence, to outdo the storm that is raging around us. I tried to induce him to take a kelladone but he refused."

"Is that all?" I asked him. "My God, man, we're all mad out here in this tempest!"

"Oh—go back to sleep!" he exclaimed, turning away in disgust.

I rolled over and tried to, but sleep was gone. I listened to the wind howl and the sounds of our movements, and then I was in the midst of this Steve-Georgia situation and worrying about what Rufe Howard had just told me.

I stuck my head out of the curtains and looked forward. Rufe was just sitting down in the navigator's seat. In front of him I could make out the back of Bill Wernecke's head. Gabe Harrow was in the co-pilot's seat—he seemed to be spending most of his time in the control cabin either piloting or watching. The glow from the Maser Screen cast a greenish tint on the side of his face and on his bald head.

Over to the right in the communications cabin was Florence Donner's red hair. Standing in the doorway was Jack Osborne, facing my way and apparently listening to something she was saying.

In the seat behind communications, across from Rufe, was Steve and Georgia. They were slumped down in the seat and I could just see the tops of their heads. I debated getting up and talking to them—trying to find out what was disturbing Rufe. Then I decided not to. Some other time, I told myself.

I was just about to lie back down when a sudden motion forward arrested my attention. I didn't realize what I had seen for an instant, then I knew it had been Steve Engles' arm, suddenly raised and then swung downward with great speed and force. I swung out of the bunk fast and started up the aisle. Jack Osborne was standing, frozen, a look of horror on his face. I could see Steve's back above the back of the seat but nothing else. He seemed to be bending over Georgia. Florence Donner's face suddenly rose up from the booth and her mouth was open as though she were screaming. No sound could be heard.

On the other side of the aisle Rufe Howard was on his feet and moving toward Steve. I was halfway the length of the snowmobile when Steve suddenly straightened up. He moved fast, giving Rufe a straight-arm that toppled him over, then brushing past Jack Osborne and knocking him into the communications cabin.

Steve grabbed the forward converter out of its bracket and pointed it in my direction as I reached the control cabin.

"Stop this God damned machine!" he bellowed.

Bill Wernecke pressed the "Stop" button and forward motion ceased. This automatically unlocked the door on the right side, toward which Steve had been backing slowly. I glanced over my right shoulder at the seat behind communications. Georgia was crouched in the corner, her head bowed down. Her black hair had fallen over her face and one bare, white arm lay across the seat. She was very still.

I looked back at Steve. He was turning the door handle behind him with his left hand, his right still holding the converter. His face was absolutely blank, his eyes unseeing, and I had the uncomfortable feeling of looking at a dead man. I started to move toward him and he pointed the converter at me again, still unseeing. I stopped moving.

Rufe Howard had regained his feet and was standing still by the navigation table, his right hand gripping the edge. He looked at me briefly, then behind me at Georgia. Bill Wernecke and Gabe Harrow sat still in their seats. Jack Osborne was standing beside Florence Donner in the communications booth, both looking at Steve.

Suddenly Steve swung the door open on its two-way hinges and a blast of icy wind almost knocked me over. I grabbed an upright for balance and saw Steve start out. He threw the converter on the floor as he vanished into the storm.

I grabbed a helmet and gloves from a rack to my left and put them on. I was wearing my arctics and I turned up the heat. I didn't bother with boots. I picked up the converter from the floor and went out into the storm after him.

I hadn't gone a few yards—or perhaps only a few feet—when I suddenly came to my senses and asked myself the question. This question was, "What in hell am I doing out in the storm hunting for a dead man?"

My chances of finding him were zero. He could have been two feet from me in any direction and he would have been as safe from my finding him as though he were a thousand miles away.

What's the matter with you? I asked myself. Are you stir-crazy, too? What are you trying to prove?

I turned 180 degrees and started to crawl. I wasn't cold—you don't get cold in Fincham arctics—but I was awfully tired and I found that the converter weighed 200 pounds. Maybe 400. There was nothing but blackness. The only directions were up and down. I don't know how long I crawled, fighting the solid blasts of wind, or how far. It seemed like forever. Then I stopped and I was looking at the lights of the snowmobile. One moment there had been inky blackness, the next lights. I tried to move toward the lights and something unyielding impeded my progress. I put my hand down. It seemed to be a log. I took off my glove and felt. I felt hair and a face, hard and cold, as though it had been sculpted out of ice.

I moved around the obstruction and I knocked on the door of the snowmobile with the converter nozzle. Bill Wernecke opened the door and lifted me inside.

"Find anything?" he asked.

I shook my head. "Nothing. Just snow."

CHAPTER NINE

THE WIND HOWLED, the snow swirled, the storm raged. But we were near St. Louis Complex and we all felt entirely different. It must have been our closeness to other human beings, the sudden end of the fearful knowledge of being alone and isolated in our inimical world. The air around us was filled with VHF and UHF broadcasting and all of our receivers were on full blast. There were smiles on faces and friendly conversations among our seventeen survivors. Even Georgia Lawrence, quickly recovered from the attack by Steve, had gotten out of her bunk and was acting friendly and pleasant. She wore the bandage Rufe Howard had fixed over her left eye and there were black marks on her neck, but she seemed unaware of her appearance, which was a rare thing for her.

There had been a sort of service for Steve Engles two nights before, after Rufe had cared for Georgia. We had not started up yet, seemingly reluctant to leave this unmarked spot in the storm where we had lost another member of our group. We all felt that something had to be said, some gesture of finality had to be made before we pushed on.

Gabe Harrow had accepted this duty with unspoken agreement. He stood by the control station and started to speak, then realized his words were being drowned out by the wind. Bill Wernecke handed him the intercom mike.

"One more of us has gone," he said. "We will miss Steve Engles and his contributions to the safety and the comfort of all. Let us pray that he has found the peace which he sought so desperately—which he couldn't find among us."

There had been no tears. We were all far beyond any such manifestations of emotion. Certainly Georgia Lawrence, lying in the dark of her bunk in the rear, would have been the last to mourn her former lover. I had passed her bunk after we had got underway again and she had put out her bandaged head.

"What was that all about?" she had asked.

"It was for Steve," I had replied.

"I could hear that. I hope the bastard burns in hell! Look what he did to me!"

The closer we approached St. Louis Complex the more stations came in until the air was a bedlam—a wonderful, welcome, heart-warming bedlam.

I told Florence Donner, "See if you can pick out a Government station from this mess of noise. Tell them who we are and where we are and ask them if they have any means by which we may get down to the City."

I took over the navigation from Rufe Howard and started the search for surface irregularities and snowdrifts in the Maser Screen. Only one drift of any size showed up. The rest of the snowscape was filled with small hummocks and flat plains. Florence came out of the communications booth, her green eyes flashing with excitement.

"I just talked to the Federal Supervisor of DW-three," she said. "Hilary Crouch. He told me Luke Hobson is in St. Louis and now heads the local Government."

I called Gabe Harrow from the co-pilot's seat and told him what Florence had reported. He sat on the edge of the navigation desk and nodded. "Sure," he said, "Luke lives in St. Louis. Been to his place many times."

"That arrest order is still out for you!" exclaimed Florence. "The minute I mentioned your name, Crouch told me about it. He said the Secretary promises to move heaven and earth to put you in prison!"

"This Crouch sounds friendly," said Gabe. "What ails him?"

"He monitored the circuits when you made your first report to Gamberelli a year ago and also for two conferences later and he says your Greenberg Theory has proved to be right after all."

"What's the situation below?" I asked.

"Very critical," she replied. "The ice has been moving for several weeks and has destroyed more than half of their remaining shelters. They've been fighting it with Cory converters and even reactor core explosions, Crouch said. They thought they had the movement arrested six days ago, but it has started again."

"Can we get down to them?" I asked.

"Crouch said it would not be advisable. He said the Lincoln Tower is still intact but may go at any hour."

I located the Lincoln Tower on a city map and plotted our own position as closely as possible with the Dace Recorder and Haverwood Navigator. I crossed to the communications booth and told Florence to get me the street locations of three of the VHF and UHF stations. By triangulation I was able to place our snowmobile within a few feet. We were nine yards southwest of Municipal Common. But that solved nothing because the snowdrift was still 8 degrees, 47 minutes too far off.

I gave Bob Jordan, at the controls, the course for the tower, which was 1,600 yards away, and at exactly 1,587 yards we arrived at a hummock so slight that the Maser Screen had not picked it up. We continued into the hummock at very slow speed, our forward converters melting out the snow ahead. Twelve yards further along we uncovered the metal roof of the tower.

The Lincoln Tower was 992 feet tall, so that was the depth of the snow over the center of St. Louis Complex on March 31st. It was the most modern building in the Complex, constructed entirely of Cresidium alloy and blocks of Bitriel, both products of Boren Industries in Missouri Center.

I asked Florence to try to raise Hilary Crouch for me again and he was on the air immediately.

"This is Colonel Savage, Commander of the Harrow Group," I said. "We are at the top of the Lincoln Tower. Can you tell me the condition of the ice at the base of the tower at this moment?"

"Hello, Colonel," said Crouch, his voice warm and friendly, in sharp contrast to those we had heard at Franklin City. "It's a pleasure to talk to you. Our latest report from that area is several hours old. At that time there was general movement of the ice and the condition of the tower was considered precarious. The Government has issued an official order against your using the tower."

"The Government moves fast in St. Louis," I said.

"I had to report your position and that you had inquired about the tower," he said. "The order was issued by Secretary Hobson, who has taken over here in the emergency. I've informed almost a hundred of our group that you are on top of the snow and there is tremendous excitement. Finley Black has gone to see the Secretary to try to arrange for you to send a party down to the Complex."

"Who is your group and who is Finley Black?" I asked.

Crouch laughed. "We're sort of rebels," he said. "The Very Reverend Dr. Black is our leader—wait a minute! I've got to get off this channel. It's Government. I'll call you in a minute on twenty-twelve megacycles."

I tuned in all of the receivers to Crouch's channel so that our entire company could hear. He was back on the air in thirty seconds.

"The Government's position is that the storms will end within two weeks and that conditions will quickly return to normal," he said. "They broadcast the hourly predictions of Curran and Vidal and their own expert here, Crosley Farmer. Any activities countering this Government view are considered treason. However, Dr. Black has enough influence so that he's kept us out of trouble. He supports the predictions of Dr. Harrow, Professor Jordan, and Carlos Ferrari who foresee an Ice Age of extended duration."

"Have you any plans?" I cut in. "Are you doing anything to escape?"

"We have several vehicles under construction. Morley Lovejoy, chief engineer at Martinson, designed them. We've had great difficulty finding parts. Also, we haven't solved the problem of getting them to the top of the snow, when they are built... We want to go south, Colonel, as your group is doing."

"We'll have to get down to you and give you our help," I said. "William Wernecke of Boren Industries is with us and he says the Lincoln Tower will withstand tremendous pressure from the ice."

"Is that a fact?" exclaimed Crouch. "Let me reach Dr. Black. We'll get that Government order rescinded."

"Tell him to get crews with converters working at the base of the tower," I said. "They can melt out the ice in the bad spots and keep off the pressure."

"I'll do what I can," he reported. "Please stand by."

Gabe Harrow, Jack Osborne and Bob Jordan were elated by this development. The entire company, in fact, seemed to feel a surge of optimism at our first encounter with persons who felt as we did and who were seeking our assistance and advice. It was a fact that we were no longer alone.

In half an hour Hilary Crouch called on the VHF and reported that the Government order against our using the Lincoln Tower had been rescinded, but that we would use it at our own risk.

"Two converter crews will work on the ice at the base of the tower," he said.

"How did you achieve all that?" I asked him.

"Dr. Black did it," he said. "He's a very persuasive man, Colonel. However, he could not persuade the Secretary to permit Dr. Harrow to accompany your party."

Gabe came to the communications booth. He poked me in the shoulder with a finger and said, "Give me that microphone."

"This is Gabriel Harrow," he said. "I'm coming down with our party. You tell that to Luke Hobson. I've played too much poker with him not to recognize one of his bluffs. You tell him I'm calling this bluff—that he doesn't scare me one bit!"

CHAPTER TEN

AT 1:30 P.M. on April first, 2204, a party composed of Dr. Harrow, Professor Osborne, Dr. Jordan, Bill Wernecke, Fred and Sam Houston Lawrence and myself removed a section of the Bitriel blocks with a converter to gain entry to the Lincoln Tower. We found the lights and heat on and the elevators operating. We descended to the main lobby in a matter of minutes and were met there by a cheering delegation numbering a score.

We had left Rufe Howard and Perry Lawrence at the top of the building equipped with converter, FX phone and the sound detector, which Bill had rigged up to one of the main vertical cresidium beams. The detector would warn immediately of any unusual or critical strains on the structure, and they could then call our party by phone.

We brought with us a copy of the original plans drawn by Rance Goodrich of our snowmobile and a complete list of the supplies and tools that we carried.

After introducing ourselves and shaking hands all around, we were led from the building lobby by Finley Black, a huge bear of a man with a shock of gray hair and a bulbous nose. Dr. Black walked with Gabe Harrow and treated Gabe with deference, much as that of pupil and master. I heard him say to Gabe, "This is the most memorable moment of my life, Dr. Harrow. You do us all great honor by coming down to us in our miserable caverns... I delivered your message to Secretary Hobson."

Gabe laughed. "What did the old coot say?" he asked.

Dr. Black shook his huge head. "Nothing. He was very angry but he said nothing."

Hilary Crouch, small and dapper, walked beside me and pointed out one of the work parties outside attacking the ice with converters. They had rigged a sluiceway so that the water went into the building basement. We entered a tunnel ten feet wide and seven high, supported by metal beams. It was well lighted and the impression it gave was of efficient and competent workmanship. About a hundred yards along, however, we came to a section badly cracked and out of line.

"All of this section caved in due to ice movement," Crouch explained. "We had just finished clearing it away when you contacted us. It was fortunate or we wouldn't have been able to reach Lincoln Tower."

We came to a tunnel running at right angles, made a left turn and entered a building ten yards farther along.

"This is the Municipal Courts Building," Crouch said. "It's one of the many buildings we shored up to withstand the weight of the snow. Dr. Black persuaded the Government to let us use it."

We were escorted through a throng of people to the far side of the vaulted lobby where a raised platform had been constructed. The crowd was silent but appeared to me to be very friendly. Most were smiling and I wondered if our presence had given them a new hope.

"We have already told you about this party of travelers from the top of the snow," said Finley Black. "Let me introduce them to you—the first strangers to visit us since the storms began. This is Colonel Savage, leader of the group. This is Dr. Gabriel Harrow, the noted scientist, and on his right are Professor Osborne and Dr. Jordan of the Mount Hood Observatory, and these two others beside

Colonel Savage are Fred and Sam Houston Lawrence, sons of a Kansas farmer. The man on the end is William Wernecke, engineer of Boren Industries.

"Most of those among you know a great deal about Dr. Harrow. He was among the first of the many who predicted that this storm engulfing the earth would be unending. As long as a year ago Dr. Harrow warned our Government and other Governments of the world of the approaching storm and its probable duration and he urged that the most drastic emergency measures be taken at once.

"Dr. Harrow, Colonel Savage, Professor Osborne, Dr. Jordan and William Wernecke are here to give us vital information. I believe Dr. Harrow will address you first."

Gabe unfolded his lanky form slowly and spoke briefly in a low, even voice; "I understand that most of you here accept the theory that the world has entered the Fifth Ice Age and that these storms will be unending during the span of years allotted to us.

"The violent winds of today should continue no longer than another fourteen years. They may end any time within these fourteen years, but exactly when I do not know. My guess is that the wind will die down toward the end of the seventh year. The snow will continue, however, at least for the next 122 years.

"Some time before next August a definite pattern of temperature and precipitation will begin to form. The one feature of vital interest is that the weather will moderate in a belt around the Earth and the temperatures in this belt will rise. It appears certain that this belt will form around the Equator. The Equatorial temperatures will vary between plus thirty and plus forty degrees Fahrenheit. The farther North one goes the colder it will get. At the Poles it would be about eighty below zero.

"It behooves us all to make our plans now and to be ready to be on our way to the Equator to meet this warmer weather. We can survive in no other way.

"This entire continent is being covered by a vast glacier. Now, glaciers do not stand still; they flow. And when they flow they carry everything before them—even mountains that get in their way. You know how it will crush your buildings and make human life impossible. If you are to survive, you must get out to the surface and you must start for the Equator."

Gabe turned abruptly and resumed his seat. There was a dead silence for several minutes. Then the throng suddenly became vocal. Voices were raised, asking the questions that Gabe had left unanswered: "How do we get out?" "What do we do?" "When do we leave?" "Tell us how!"

Dr. Black raised his hand for attention. He turned to me and said, "Colonel Savage, will you answer the questions of these people?"

I described our snowmobile in detail and then held up the copy of the plans. "We will leave these with you," I said. "We will help you in any other way that we can."

I told them how we had constructed our tunnel-ramp from Harrow farm and how we had attached a thrust-engine to our vehicle to help us get out. I then described our trip of some 200 miles and told them of our mishaps with the soft snow areas and the winds.

I concluded by telling them of our plan to go to Norfolk Complex and there attempt to put a boat into commission to carry us south.

"We've had enough talk!" exclaimed one man, waving his hand from the rear of the crowd. "Let us get to work now and save ourselves!"

This brought general cries of agreement as I sat down. Finley Black stood up. "With the help of our friends," he said, "who have come to us out of the storm, perhaps we can accomplish more than we have to date."

A cheer went up as Dr. Black turned away. The men and women of the audience then began to form into groups, each group with a leader. Our party gathered around Dr. Black, and he asked me if we could come with them to the factory they had set up for the construction of their snow vehicles. I had just agreed and we were moving to the stairway from the platform when there was a commotion at the rear and someone shouted, "The police are here!"

We stopped and looked over the heads of the crowd. Two uniformed men were moving through the groups towards us followed by a short, fat man in civilian clothes who was Luke Hobson, Secretary for Internal Affairs.

The three came to the foot of the platform and Hobson pointed a finger at Gabe Harrow. "That's the man," he said to the officers. "Arrest him."

The officers mounted the stairs to the platform. Bill Wernecke picked up our converter from the floor and moved to the edge of the platform where he would have everybody within range. I went to Dr. Black's side.

I gestured toward Bill Wernecke and the converter. "We do not propose to permit you to arrest Dr. Harrow, Mr. Hobson."

He glared at me out of ice-blue eyes, then glanced at Bill Wernecke.

"How dare you threaten me!" he exclaimed.

"We have dared the storms on the surface and your blustering is nothing," I said. "Order your policemen to release Dr. Harrow."

"I will do no such thing!" he exclaimed.

Dr. Black had been following this exchange with a look of amusement on his face. "It looks as if you will have to do what Colonel Savage requires, Mr. Secretary," he said.

"Gabriel Harrow is a traitor!" declared Hobson. He slapped the warrant in his hand.

I jumped down to the floor and faced Hobson. "When you've made it stop snowing with your asinine Government decrees, then you can arrest Dr. Harrow," I said. "Meanwhile, I'll take this."

I snatched the warrant from his hand and tore it up. Much of the crowd on the floor had gathered closely around us and there were cries of approval at my action. Hobson looked around at their faces, all hostile to him, and he seemed to shrink to half his plump size.

"I'll call out the entire police force if I have to!" said the Secretary. "I insist that the law be enforced!"

"And I insist that we be permitted to depart in peace," I said. "I will give you five seconds to order the release of Dr. Harrow, then we go into action. Bill, get your converter ready. One-two-three-four—"

"Wait!" yelled Hobson. "You two officers, release Dr. Harrow. We will return to City Hall and organize properly for this duty."

The two officers walked off the platform, evidently happy to get out of the mess. Hobson tried to push his way through the crowd to meet them, but the bodies were unyielding. He began to flay his arms, and a large and placid-looking man with a full beard put his arms around him and held him fast.

"You want me to do anything with this type?" he asked me.

"No, just hold him here until my party and I can return to the top of the snow. Give us about twenty minutes."

"You are leaving us?" exclaimed Dr. Black in dismay.

"I think it would be best for all of us," I replied. "Hobson will not give up. Personally, I think he's become psychopathic and I'm certain he would be a danger to all of you if we remained to stimulate his anger further."

Dr. Black grasped my hand. I think there were tears in his eyes. But maybe not.

CHAPTER ELEVEN

THE WOMAN STOPPED US as we were leaving the Courts Building. We learned later that she was Mrs. Helen Livingstone. She was standing on the steps with two children in their teens, both of them scrubbed and neat. She was cold and she shivered often despite her will to control it.

"May I speak to you a moment, Colonel Savage?" she asked, putting an ungloved hand on my arm.

I gave her what I hoped was an encouraging smile.

"I heard your talk—the children and I heard you," she said with great urgency. "We all liked you and your people and we know of your great kindness in coming down to us to try to help us...Have you room for my two children in your snowmobile?"

Gabe Harrow, Bill Wernecke and Dr. Black had come back to us to find out what was delaying me, and they stood looking at her with sympathy.

"I am afraid that your suggestion is not practical, madam," said Dr. Black. "We can hardly ask these kind people to be directly responsible for any of us."

"But I do not ask for myself!" she cried. "It is for Dennis and Bettina! They are so young, Dr. Black, and they should have a chance to live!"

"You would send your children away with us?" asked Gabe Harrow.

"Oh, yes! I would do anything to get them away from this certain death beneath the snow!"

I looked at the children, Bettina, 14, and Dennis, 13. Their faces were prematurely old, showing already lines of worry and strain.

"We have room in our vehicle," I said. "Do your children want to come with us?"

"They have talked of nothing else since we first heard you were on top of the snow!" she replied.

"And what would you do?" I asked. "We have room for three. All of you join us."

"I must take care of my husband," she said. "His back was broken when our building collapsed. He has very little time to live. But take the children, please."

I turned to Gabe and Bill Wernecke. They both nodded.

"All right," I told her.

She sank to her knees and buried her head in her arms. The children looked at her, embarrassed.

"Say goodbye to your mother," I told them. "We haven't much time."

"Yes, sir," said the boy. The two of them knelt down and put their arms around her. "Goodbye, Mommy," they said in her ear. Then they jumped up and came to my side.

We started on. I looked back and I saw the woman still huddled on the steps, her face hidden in her arms.

CHAPTER TWELVE

WE STAYED at the roof of Lincoln Tower for the next two days, in constant touch by radio with Dr. Black, Hilary Crouch, the engineer Morley Lovejoy and others of their group, giving them what help and advice we could. I like to think that we were at least partially responsible for the completion of their snow vehicles and for their eventual escape to the South.

A not inconsiderable obstacle was the opposition of Luke Hobson. He attempted to delay them in every way possible during the weeks immediately following our visit. It was this period that was the most critical for them because the glacial movement was increasing hourly, imperiling all of their efforts. Dr. Black and his people fought back, of course, but they were not supplied with their final and most effective weapon until the time had passed when the snow should have stopped and the thaw set in, according to the predictions of Curran and Vidal and Farmer, and supported by Hobson and the Government.

When the snow did not stop and the thaw did not set in, Hobson lost all of his supporters and finally his authority. Hobson was summarily ousted from his position as Director—we learned later—and was found a suicide a few hours after this debacle in his barred apartment in City Hall.

We left the vicinity of St. Louis Complex on April third shortly before midnight, when Hobson's police came to the top of Lincoln Tower armed with converters. Their primary mission was to seize Dr. Harrow, but it appeared they would be satisfied if they could drive us away. We had set up a communications room at the top of the tower and this was manned by Sam Houston Lawrence and Georgia when the police arrived.

Georgia contacted me immediately by FX phone and gave me the news. "We are under arrest," she said. "Six policemen are up here. They demand that you produce Dr. Harrow."

"Let me talk to the officer in charge," I told her.

A Lieutenant Clayborne came on the phone and delivered his ultimatum to me. "We are armed with converters," he said. "We mean business."

"Two converters on our machine," I replied, "are now aimed at the tower directly under you. I shall turn them on and destroy your means of descent and escape unless you release our two people at once."

There was a long pause. "Will you leave the area of the Complex immediately if I release the prisoners?" he said.

"We will depart immediately then," I said. "We have done all we can to help those below."

"I know you have," said the Lieutenant, his voice softening. "Good luck to you all."

Sam Houston and Georgia came back aboard carrying their equipment and we backed away from Lincoln Tower. We kept the St. Louis Complex stations on the air as long as we were in range and continued to talk to our friends. I had a final talk with Dr. Black twenty days later, just before the last station dimmed out. He told me briefly of their difficulties with the Government people, wished us Godspeed, and then gave me a message for the Livingstone children. Their father had died. Their mother sent them her love.

CHAPTER THIRTEEN

TWO HUNDRED AND FIFTY MILES to the east lay the huge Kentucky Complex, which had been before the storms the most important industrial center South of Michigan Complex and Chicago Complex. Historians are aware that Kentucky Complex was erected on the site of the old City of Louisville, which was a community of no particular consequence in the Dark Centuries. There were no cities of any size on our route between St. Louis Complex and Kentucky, so we made the latter our next goal.

We left St. Louis Complex in much higher spirits than at any time since our start from Fallon, despite the discouraging experience there. We felt we had accomplished something of value to fellow human beings. Another thing that gave us a tremendous lift was the two Livingstone children, and we took them to our hearts immediately, without reservations. Here were two young humans who needed us just as desperately as we needed them.

There had been no change in the weather. While we had been at Lincoln Tower, Fred Lawrence had cleaned out the McMillan wind gauge and had constructed a screen over the vent, which would prevent the snow from clogging it. The screen cut down the velocity reading by some fifteen per cent, but he had had the acumen to measure his reduction accurately so that the actual velocity could be computed. Thus, we knew now how hard the wind was blowing. Over St. Louis Complex as we departed it had been 89 miles per hour out of the West. Two hours later the velocity had risen to 92 miles per hour.

The snow continued at about the same rate, as near as we could judge. Our only reliable yardstick was the visibility, and that remained at the same several feet as at the outset.

So the wind howled and the snowmobile shook and swayed and the solid wall of white was always around us, but gone completely was the utter depression and the helpless apathy of the previous period of endless miles.

The changes brought about by this new mood seemed to me to be dramatic and out of all proportion to the reality. The outward difference was no more than a smile or a pleasant word, but I had the feeling of friendship and warmth and, even more important, that we could rely upon each other to the ultimate for our safety and well being.

Now even Georgia Lawrence appeared occasionally to have joined us and to have become a part of our body. Over St. Louis Complex she had finally emerged and had reassumed her regular watch on communications. After she had returned to our vehicle with her brother from Lincoln Tower and we had got under way again, she had suddenly begun to talk cheerfully to the rest of us. For the next eight weeks as we crawled painfully and fitfully towards Kentucky Complex, she made not one disagreeable remark to any of us. But I continued to retain my basic doubts about her, and I developed a feeling of most peculiar certainty that she was our bad luck and that she would somehow cause us disaster.

It took us 57 days to negotiate the 250 miles from St. Louis Complex to Kentucky Complex. It seemed that the further east we got the more difficult our progress. The areas of soft snow became so frequent and of such wide extent that we were continually detouring to north and south, and the actual mileage we covered between these two points was 633.

I have examined my journal carefully for this period, as well as the notes of Dr. Harrow, and I can find nothing of interest to comment upon beyond a few paragraphs about radio reception and several of the stations we talked to.

Generally the VHF and UHF reception was very bad and of limited scope. It was Professor Osborne's theory, as reported by Gabe Harrow, that the Heaviside Layer, which normally reflected the radio waves back to Earth and thus kept them from vanishing into space, had receded to such a high altitude that it was no longer effective. We spent several days attempting to contact the Space Platforms to verify this, but our efforts were not productive. Our one receiver that we could tune to the Platform frequencies (it was against the law for individuals to possess such receivers) had very early burned out a vital coil and condenser, and Fred Lawrence's attempt to replace these with parts from other receivers had produced signals that were so faint that they were generally undecipherable. We determined that we were in contact with Plymouth 21 Platform but little else.

Then on May 17th and 18th, for no explainable reason other than a possible sudden shifting of the Heaviside Layer, the high frequency reception became almost normal and we spent forty hours in conversations with persons all over the world. Florence Donner, Jack Osborne, Georgia Lawrence, Rufe Howard, Bill Wernecke and I stayed awake almost this entire period monitoring broadcasts and speaking to survivors of the storm.

Only once did we contact a group of travelers on top of the snow such as we, making their slow and precarious way through Europe West to the Atlantic. They identified themselves as the DiMaestri Party and they seemed as depressed as we had been on our leg from Missouri Center to

St. Louis Complex. We tried to give them cheer and hope but they would have none of it. Nor did they want to talk to us or to listen to us. They would not tell us their plans, beyond saying they hoped to put a boat into commission and get out to sea.

The most significant bit of information we picked up was in a broadcast from Freetown, Africa West, that gave a complete weather report from that area. On May 18th the temperature there was 20 degrees Fahrenheit—the warmest reported from anywhere on Earth up to that time—the wind was 48 knots, and the snowfall was estimated at a little over an inch per hour.

I tried for four hours to contact this station on our own sender but they would not answer—perhaps due to bad reception. I wanted desperately to ask them when the temperature had started to rise and at what rate it was warming up, for this was our first clue that Gabe Harrow's prediction of warmer weather in the Equatorial Belt was beginning to come about.

CHAPTER FOURTEEN

WE CONTACTED three UHF radio stations at Kentucky Complex on May 17th and 18th and we learned that conditions in the industrial metropolis were almost unbelievably bad.

One of the stations we talked to was a semi-official Government operation. We became well acquainted with its operator, George Farrell, former DW-three supervisor and a friend of Hilary Crouch in St. Louis Complex. He was located at the center of the Complex on Government Square and he told us that there were no more than 500 people left alive in this small area which remained intact.

"But the ice is moving in on us, a few more inches every day, so it won't be long now," he said during an early conversation. "We had a ramp built to the surface a month ago and we have two machines that can travel on top of the snow, but they will hold only about fifty persons, and no one has been willing to take the responsibility of designating the fifty who would go in them. We have let the ramp deteriorate while we argued about this."

Gabe Harrow and Rufe Howard talked to Farrell and urged him to force a decision on the use of their snow vehicles before it was too late. Rufe Howard told him the passengers should be selected by age; that only the youngest should be taken and that the passenger list should be made up arbitrarily along those lines.

Farrell said he agreed in principle, but he said he could not suggest it because he was only twenty-six and would surely be one of those to go.

"Our difficulty is not jealousy and self-interest," he explained. "We are a small group now and we have become fast friends. We can't think of abandoning each other. We need an arbitrator—someone with enough strength and authority to tell us what to do and force us to do it."

A second station we contacted at the Complex was operated by an amateur, one Flora Dickinson, who said she was in her early twenties but "looked like a mess." She said she and forty-two others were living in a tunnel under the old railroad station and that it seemed secure enough to last forever.

"We've got a couple of reactors and plenty of fuel and a good oxygen generator and several tons of food concentrates—but we are all sitting down here and dying just the same," she said. "If we cannot escape—if we can never live on top of the world again, what's the use of living at all?"

What could I say to her?

Marge had been listening to our conversation and came up to the communication booth.

"Give me that mike a moment," she said. "I want to talk to that girl."

I handed her the mike and she said, "This is one of the Savage Company (it was the first time that designation was used for us) and I've been hearing your complaints up here on top of the snow. You give me a pain in the neck, Flora Dickinson, sitting down there and crying the blues. Of course life isn't pleasant any more! No dances and no boy friends and no dates up in the stars, flying around in your own Ring with your favorite male. It's all grim and cold and difficult, but that's no reason to give up! You've got your friends down in that tunnel, haven't you? You've got heat and light and food and you can live safely for years, as you yourself admit. So live it, girl, and see if you can't make something more out of it than misery for yourself and your companions!"

"Wow!" exclaimed Flora Dickinson, "I guess I asked for that! And who are you and how are you making out?"

"This is Marge Savage," she replied, "and we're making out fine. Of course the wind is blowing and you can't see more than a few feet in any direction because of the snow, but there are nineteen of us and we're alive today, which is the main point."

"I guess," the girl replied, "if you can stand it, I can... Well, it was nice to have talked to another woman. I'm the only girl with our party."

"You're sitting down there with forty guys and you're complaining?"

"Maybe I could fix my hair," said Flora Dickinson.

The third Kentucky station we contacted was manned by a group of professionals who said they had operated a VM station before the storm. They were in a large industrial plant on the outskirts of the Complex with 250 others, living in two buildings that had been shored up early to withstand the weight of the snow. The buildings were constructed entirely of Lomax metal and had withstood the pressure of the ice, although twisted out of shape and pushed upward nearly 20 feet. They had one Cory converter that they had kept operating day and night to combat the ice at the critical points, and so far had been able to keep ahead of it.

The leader of this group identified himself as Wiley Baylor, former director of the VM station.

"I don't know what the Hell we're doing down here or why," he told me. "We continue our daily fight to live, but there's no point in it because we can't win. Sooner or later the ice will catch up with us, just as it's caught up with practically all of the millions who once lived in the Complex. But it's good to hear a human voice from on top of the snow and to know that there are men and women who have figured out a way to beat this."

I questioned him at length and I had to admit it seemed hopeless. They had no way of constructing any sort of vehicle, although they had enough reactors to power a hundred of them. In fact, the energy they had at their command was almost unlimited, for one of the buildings they were in had been used to store the finished reactors and various reactor-powered tools.

Bill Wernecke took over the microphone then and started to question Baylor about the tools and machines available. Baylor described what was in the place as best he could, but he explained he was no engineer, nor was any member of their party, and they didn't know what half of the gadgets lying about could be used for.

"There's one place to go that you haven't thought of," said Bill. "That's down. What you've got to do is to find some digging tools. Haven't you got anybody there at all who knows about tools?"

"Nobody," said Baylor. "We've got accountants and a barber and five lady dancers who were on our VM station; clerks, computer operators—people like that."

"All right," said Bill, "This is what a Davey Digger looks like. The business end is a bundle of pipes, each about four inches in diameter, and the whole some four feet across. At the tail end the chassis tapers to a single pipe with a diameter of six or seven inches. There are two handles in the middle. Actually it resembles a huge funnel. Now have you seen anything like that lying about?"

"Oh yes," said Baylor. "There are several of them in crates. There is a lot of flexible pipe with them. What's that for?"

"That's for the exhaust, which spews out the materials you dig up," said Bill. "You attach the flexible pipe on the rear end, then keep away from it. The stuff comes out fast and hot. You rest your digger on the ground, or against a wall or any place you want to make a hole, press the green switch under the little cover between the two handles, and it goes to work. It'll dig through anything—rock, metal, dirt. You stop it with the red switch. Is that all clear?"

"It is," said Baylor.

"Fine. Now put them to work. You'll be able to dig yourselves a cavern big enough to have a room of your own, each. But go down deep, man. This ice is powerful stuff."

"You've just saved the lives of a lot of very grateful people," said Baylor, his voice charged with emotion. "We'll never forget you!"

Bill Wernecke put the microphone down and gave me a wry smile. "Maybe they won't," he said. "But it's more likely they'll live to damn us for prolonging their agony... What a life that's going to be, down in a hole under the frozen ground!"

CHAPTER FIFTEEN

ON MAY 18TH at around 7:30 P.M. the radio reception started to fade and within half an hour more than 90 per cent of the stations we had been able to contact were out of our range. We were left with five code stations, which broadcast some news and weather but would not answer our calls to give us specific requested information, and one voice station from Mexico Province that occasionally would come in clear and then fade to nothing. Our snowmobile routine went back to normal for travel, which was an hour-to-hour and day-to-day preoccupation with any small task or game or avocation that would pass the time.

A strange and unexpected friendship grew up quickly between Bettina and Georgia and it was disturbing to both Marge and myself. I couldn't have said why, but Marge expressed some of my apprehension when she said that Bettina had apparently formed a girlish "crush" for Georgia, considering her beautiful and talented.

"My God," I said, "I hope she doesn't try to model her life on the Lawrence girl's!"

"She will for now, but only superficially," said Marge. "She'll dress like her and fix her hair like hers—but don't worry about the rest of it. This Bettina is a smart little girl and she'll discover Georgia's weaknesses soon enough. Wait until Georgia throws her next tantrum and she'll drop her like a reactor plug."

On May 27th, when we were far north of Kentucky Complex due to a long and arduous detour around a great soft snow area, we brought in the Complex stations again and renewed our friendships with Farrell, Flora Dickinson and Wiley Baylor. The group in Government Square had abandoned their apathy and were working once more on their tunnel-ramp up to the surface which, Farrell said, was almost completed. They had decided to select fifty-two of their number to follow us in their two snow vehicles. He reported that a Harvey Lewishon, engineer, had assumed command of the survivors and was administering matters with a firm hand.

There was no change in the physical situation of the group in the tunnel under the old railway station, but Flora Dickinson sounded like an entirely different girl, and there was little of the hopelessness and depression in her voice that we had heard before, nor in the voices of other members of the group we talked to. Both Marge and I were curious about how Flora Dickinson had worked out her personal problem, but she refused to discuss it or to give us any hint, even. Marge talked to her for almost a half an hour, with zero results.

"I think she's picked one of those forty men," Marge told me later. "Or maybe she's picked several of them... What a life!"

We couldn't raise the Baylor station at all until around midnight of the 27th, but both Farrell and Flora told us they were in regular contact with this group. "They've gone away underground," Flora said. "They've dug themselves a vast apartment down deep and their radio doesn't work too well from there. They also found an entrance to one of the old railway tunnels and one of these days they're going to explore it and see if it won't lead them to us. It should, you know, because we're down under the old station."

When finally we talked to Wiley Baylor we learned that there were only 98 of them left—that the rest had been caught in the collapse of their former residence before their underground cavern was completed.

"It's my fault," said Wiley. "It took me too long to learn how to work that Davey Digger. Also, we neglected the converter while we were digging and the ice suddenly was upon us. I guess I'm not much of an organizer."

On May 30th we arrived over Kentucky Complex. We found the entrance to the tunnel ramp without difficulty, for Harvey Lewishon had placed a pole marker there to guide us and we had picked it up in the Maser Screen five miles away.

I had Farrell on the UHF and told him we had arrived. "We will send a party down to you immediately," I said into the microphone. "In what direction does your tunnel lie? What is the compass bearing of the ramp?"

"East and west," replied Farrell. "The tunnel descends due west—we did not want to come up into the face of the wind. Colonel, there is a question we want to ask. Have you room in your vehicle for any of our people?"

"We can take four more persons," I replied immediately.

"Have you any preferences—men or women?"

"No."

"Will they need any special equipment or extra food?"

"Nothing but Fincham arctics," I said. "We're starting."

Our party was composed of Bill Wernecke, Perry Lawrence and his two sons, Jack Osborne, Bob Jordan and myself. Bill Wernecke and I took converters and each member of the party had a Bandburger torch. Fred Lawrence carried the FX phone to keep in touch with our vehicle and Florence Donner stood by on the top end of the phone.

The seven of us scrambled out of our snowmobile into the storm and crawled and stumbled to the marker. The wind was 87 miles per hour and the temperature was nine degrees below zero. It was no day to go out for a walk. I used my converter, pointing it into the wind and down, and the infrared blast melted out a huge declivity in the snow. We started into this, the converter melting away the snow ahead, and 50 feet along we were into the tunnel. I turned off the converter and we started down, our torches lighting the way. The grade was between seven and ten per cent and the roadway about 17 feet wide. The arched roof of the tunnel rose to 18 to 20 feet and was coated with a thick layer of ice. It was a well-built tunnel, larger than ours at Fallon, with the grade not as steep.

Far down the tunnel we could see lights and as we got closer a wild shouting reached our ears, the words of greeting and congratulations reverberating off the ice walls.

We all shouted back and within a few minutes we were in the midst of the work party, a group of a dozen men and women dressed in arctics, helmets and boots. It was a touching moment as they embraced us and bade us welcome and I have no doubt that there were many tears, although you couldn't be sure with the helmets.

We met Harvey Lewishon, who was in charge of the workers, a giant of a man with a deep, booming voice. He explained that they were leveling off the roadway, that their work was almost done and that they would join us below in very little time. "Our machines are all ready to go," he told me. "But please look them over. We know little about this."

"You're going with them?" I asked him.

He shook his head. "No room for old men like me," he replied. There was no note of regret in his voice.

Our seven pushed on down the ramp and we reached the bottom in another twenty minutes (their tunnel-ramp was a mile and a quarter long). Waiting for us there were all of the rest of the survivors of Government Square and they set up a cheering and bellowing that was deafening when we hove into sight.

I found George Farrell immediately and he led us to their two snowmobiles, parked side by side on the lower floor of a building across the square.

They were grotesque vehicles indeed, taller and wider than ours, although about the same length. The wheels were twelve feet in diameter and were adapted from those of earth-moving machines in mining operations. The rubber tires contained huge spikes that would dig into the ice and prevent slipping. A single reactor engine powered the two rear wheels and a second engine the front, and there was a gearbox and transmission for each pair of wheels—an antiquated arrange-ment used widely in former times.

"It'll work," said Bill Wernecke, climbing out from under-neath one of the machines. "They've got about half the power we have but they'll be okay if they can keep out of bad holes." He turned to Farrell. "Who designed these for you?"

"We inherited them from the Government," he replied. "They were all finished but the interiors and we did that work ourselves in the past few weeks."

"They're not finished yet by a long shot," said Bill. "You're going to have to have converters front and rear to melt your way out of trouble and we're going to have to run heat lines to the gear boxes and transmissions to keep them from freezing up...All right, let's get to work. Where are your tools?"

I went into the vehicles with Bob Jordan and Jack Osborne and we checked over all the equipment and supplies. There was a Maser Screen, gyrocompass and course computer in each vehicle, but they lacked torches, Corning jacks and other, power tools. I made a list of the items they should have and I gave it to Farrell.

"We can't get any of these things," he said. "Our supply stores were destroyed weeks ago."

"Then you're going to have to travel with us and keep close," I said. "If you'd get into trouble you'd be lost without tools."

"We hoped to travel with you," he replied. "Harvey Lewishon is the only one among us who even knows how to navigate and he's not going along."

"You can't venture out into the snow without navigators!"

"Well—Lewishon won't go. We picked our voyagers by age, and he's many years away."

"Find Lewishon," I said.

When Harvey Lewishon came into building and took off his helmet, he revealed a shock of white hair, black eyebrows and eyes that appeared like black jets.

I said, "As you know, Mr. Lewishon, I am commander of our group. I have examined your vehicles and I find they are lacking in tools and other equipment, so I would not consider that we travel any other way but together. Thus I am assuming command of all of the vehicles and the people in them."

"By all means, Colonel," he said. "We have been hoping and praying that that would be your decision."

"As commander of this expedition, then, I will issue my first order. You, Harvey Lewishon, are herewith appointed a deputy commander and you will occupy one of these vehicles."

He looked at me for a long moment, his eyes boring into mine. Then he shook his head slowly. "I will have to decline, Colonel," he said.

"You may not decline," I snapped. "That is an order." There was anger and chagrin in his eyes. He looked around the building, at the machines and the workers, then back to me.

Finally he asked, "May I discuss this with you?"

"Go ahead," I said.

"You are the commander. I accept that. But I urge you to give me your reason for ordering me to accompany this group."

"I am not willing to entrust these machines to the conditions that prevail on top of the snow without a competent navigator in each. If we became separated and if there was no one able to navigate, then all in that machine would perish. I will give you a navigator for one machine but I have no one I can spare for the second."

"Then I will go along of course," he said.

I had not doubted that he would accept my order, even if I had not explained.

"You would really prefer not to go?" I asked him.

"You see, Colonel, I have a wife here with me. A daughter, too, and she has been assigned to one of our vehicles, but my wife was not. Such adventures are for the young." His eyes were cast down. Then he resumed, "It is going to be most difficult to say goodbye...I shall go now and tell her, if you will excuse me."

CHAPTER SIXTEEN

IT HAD BEEN my decision that Bob Jordan—and Libby of course—would go with one of the vehicles of the Kentucky Complex survivors. Bob had become an excellent navigator besides being a fine pilot, during the long trek from St. Louis. I had a brief talk with him as the passengers were loading into the machines.

"I'll be sorry to leave our company and I know Libby will too," he said. "But I like the idea, Vic, and I know Libby will go along. We can do a lot more for this new group."

"You go aboard that one, then," I told him, indicating the, nearest snowmobile. "Pick out a couple of likely looking passengers for us and tell them that they'll transfer to our machine and why. See if you can find some Bridge players."

"Not likely!" he exclaimed. "They all look like teenagers. But you give Libby and me a couple of weeks and we'll have some of them playing."

"She'll join you when we get on top of the snow," I said, "with cards and toothbrush."

Then I turned to Lewishon, telling him to follow the Jordan vehicle as closely as possible and not to hesitate to let us know by FX phone if he was getting too far behind or had any difficulty, no matter how slight.

"I share your respect for our climate, Colonel," he said. "I had a brief look at it a couple of days ago when we broke our tunnel through at the top. Do you want your four new passengers now?"

"I should like to meet them," I said. "We'll all ride up the ramp with you and transfer to our own vehicle on top."

He beckoned to three men and a girl who had been standing to one side, watching the activity of the loading and the leave-takings. They were in their twenties and I could tell little about them from looking at them. All four seemed apprehensive, which was understandable. Two of the boys were tall and thin, the third of medium height and much too fat. The girl was quite tall—about five feet six—and carried herself with dignity and poise. She had a face that gave the impression of beauty, although on close examination her nose was too large and her mouth too broad, but you didn't notice these imperfections at all at a first glance.

"I want you to meet my daughter," said Harvey Lewishon. "This is Chriss, named after her mother, Colonel Victor Savage."

She shook hands with me and she had a grip as firm as a man's. "I'm very glad to meet you," she said as though she meant it.

Lewishon presented the three boys, Mike Haley and Jeff English, the two tall ones, and Fritz Richter, the fat one. Haley and English, I had noticed, were among those who had worked on the two snowmobiles.

"You mechanics?" I asked them.

"Just amateurs," said Haley. "I was in college majoring in economics before the storm and Jeff here was going to be a surgeon."

"How about you?" I asked Richter.

"No mechanical skills," he replied. "Just overweight. I wanted to be an actor, if ever I could have shed this pound-age."

"You'll probably shed it with us," I replied. "Food concentrates don't put on much weight."

Perry Lawrence and his two sons went to Bob Jordan's machine and Bill Wernecke, Jack Osborne, and the rest of us to go went to the other vehicle with Harvey Lewishon and George Farrell, his second in command. Harvey and his daughter walked side by side, their arms around each other. At the door of the snowmobile they stopped and spoke to an angular, gray-haired woman dressed in a black suit and leaning on a cane.

"Thought you weren't going to bother with this nonsense," said Harvey.

"I wasn't," she replied, matching his casual tone. "I just wanted to make sure Chriss Junior had on her suit of woolies... Goodbye, Harv."

He looked at her a moment, then put a hand out to her cheek. "Goodbye, Chriss," he said in a low voice, barely audible.

Young Chriss hugged and kissed her mother, then broke away and hurried into the vehicle. We all followed her in and the doors were closed. Bill Wernecke took the controls and I sat next to him and checked the instruments as he applied the power slowly and we began to move.

It is most difficult for me to describe this leave-taking from the two hundred or so survivors of Government Square. There was much good-natured banter and calling back and forth and the general spirit was that of a gay holiday, outwardly. But we were abandoning them to perish. They had no alternative. They would die in the ice.

I have often wondered since whether we weren't criminally negligent in leaving them—whether we shouldn't have packed all 200 of them into our vehicles willy-nilly without regard for the safety of the rest of us. Reason tells me that we could not have done so, that even one person over capacity of each vehicle would have been a danger to all, just as one person too many would have swamped a lifeboat at sea.

A cheer went up from the crowd as we began to move. Most of them followed us, running along side, as we crossed the Square through the large main tunnel and headed for the ramp. I looked behind and I could see Bob Jordan's lumbering vehicle following closely.

The Kentucky snowmobiles had ample power and traction to take them up the ramp. About halfway through the tunnel, however, the huge wheels began to dig down into the ice in an alarming manner and we had to reduce our speed to a bare crawl to keep from becoming mired.

I got on the FX phone to Florence Donner and told her we were within about thirty minutes of the surface.

"Have Gabe Harrow back our vehicle away from the marker," I said. "We'll come through with a final rush and we don't want any collisions. Tell him to stay close to the area and pick us up on the Maser Screen. We'll stop as soon as both machines get to the top. Tell Gabe to come alongside. We've got some people to transfer back and forth."

"Back and forth?" she asked.

"Libby and Bob Jordan are going to be with one of these machines," I said. "Tell Libby to get ready. Oh yes, and tell her to take several decks of Bridge cards."

Twenty-five minutes later we went blasting out of the tunnel and through the soft snow that had been drifted into the hole by the gale, our converter going and our huge wheels grinding away with their metal spikes. We came out into the lash of the storm and our vehicle began to shake and rattle as though it were in the mouth of an angry hound. A cry of dismay went up from our passengers and I grabbed the intercom mike.

"Get all the loose gear lashed down," I yelled over the blast of the wind. "We're up on top of the snow now and this is the way it is—violent and cold. You'll get used to it."

We made a turn of 90 degrees so that we could get Bob Jordan's machine on our Maser Screen, then came to a halt. We watched Jordan emerge from under the snow and head toward us. He came to a stop a few feet from our front wheels and we could just see the outline of his snowmobile through the storm.

Bill Wernecke, Jack Osborne and our four new group members gathered their gear and waited by the door. Lewishon, now in the pilot's seat, told us our own snowmobile was moving slowly towards us on the right.

"They're thirty feet away," he announced. "Bearing zero one five, speed about two miles per hour...Now they are twenty feet and slowing down...Here they are, ten feet to our right and stopped."

Mike Haley was standing next to me and I yelled in his ear, "Pass the word along. Follow me and don't try to stand up. Crawl. Let's go!"

I opened the door and plunged into the gale. The ten feet to our own vehicle took the energy of ten miles in normal going. Rufe Howard opened the door of our snowmobile as I arrived and helped to haul me in. I turned back and grabbed Haley's arm and dragged him aboard. He stood by my side and helped the others in—Chriss Lewishon, Bill Wernecke, Jeff English, Fritz Richter and Jack Osborne. Perry Lawrence and his two sons were right on their heels from the other machine, bringing with them the two replacements for Bob Jordan and Libby. When they were all aboard Perry introduced the last two of our complement. One was a chunky 19-year-old named Sid Garrell. He hid his fear under a brash, wisecracking exterior and his first words to me were, "Fancy buggy you got here, Doc." I let that pass and met the second of Bob Jordan's choices, a teenage blonde who claimed to be nineteen, with a flamboyant sex-ripeness. Her name was Lily Fortune and the hand she offered me was soft and damp.

I introduced our six new members over the intercom and asked Marge to take them around to our group and present them, then assign them their bunks. Libby Jordan had said her adieus meanwhile and came forward to leave. She put her arms around my neck and held her cheek to mine for a moment. "Goodbye, Vic," she said.

I opened the door for her and helped her down into the snow, then led the way to Bob's vehicle. She kept up with me without difficulty and wasn't even breathing hard when I lifted her up into the snowmobile. I waved a last goodbye to her and to Bob, standing at her side in the door, then came back.

In a very few minutes we were on our way East, now with three machines and 75 people. Gabe Harrow was at the controls and I dropped into the co-pilot's seat.

"I noticed you looking over our teenage bomb, Lily Fortune," I said.

He nodded his bald head. "I was astounded to realize that there were still such people left," he replied. "There's a little girl who's going to be bad news to a lot of men, if she can possibly manage it."

"Another Georgia?" I suggested.

"No, Lily plays in an entirely different league, strictly a lower-echelon siren—the working man's friend."

"I'm glad to see you've given the matter some thought," I said.

CHAPTER SEVENTEEN

IT WAS MAY 31ST at 9:00 A.M. that our three vehicles started out from the snow over Kentucky Complex. I told Gabe Harrow to proceed at minimum speed and to keep in touch with the Kentucky vehicles constantly for the next several hours and find out all of their peculiarities and how the wind and snow was affecting them. Then I turned in and was asleep almost immediately.

I was dreaming about snowstorms and tough teenagers (not sexy Lily) when I was shaken awake by Rufe Howard.

"We've lost one of our machines," he said in my ear. "Lewishon's snowmobile doesn't show up anywhere on our Maser Screen."

Gabe Harrow, still at the controls, told me Bob Jordan reported he had lost FX phone contact with the Lewishon machine in the middle of a conversation.

"I turned one-eighty degrees," he said, "and searched everything to the rear but there isn't a sign of it."

I located Jordan's machine on the Maser Screen and told Gabe to proceed along side. "We'll start our hunt from there," I said. "There's only one place Lewishon could be that wouldn't show up on the screen and that's down in a hole under the snow."

Georgia Lawrence, on watch in communications, had been trying to raise the snowmobile on UHF and VHF as well as by FX. There was no response on any wavelength, she reported.

I noted that young Jeff English was in the communication booth with Georgia. She had lost no time picking one of the new men, apparently. Young Jeff seemed to be in a daze and he couldn't take his eyes off her. I looked around for Lily Fortune and saw her in the rear in a seat beside Sam Houston Lawrence. Of the two girls, if I had to make a choice, I'd probably go along with Georgia and all her insanity. A girl like Lily could become deadly dull in a very short time.

The thoughts that cross your mind. Neither would have been the woman for me, or ever would be the woman that Marge was.

We stopped beside Jordan's snowmobile and I asked him on the FX if he'd veered off his course since last hearing from Lewishon and before he had stopped. He said he had not, so I told him to wait for my return and I told Gabe to start going in circles, widening them at each full turn.

At the South limit of the eleventh turn we hit an area of soft snow that dropped very suddenly and steeply and we came to a halt at a precarious angle. Gabe backed our vehicle out slowly.

"We've got to explore this crevasse in both directions from here," I told Gabe. "Try it on the west first. Go into it slowly every ten feet or so, then back out. Don't go down too deep or we'll get stuck sure."

We searched the crevasse for two hours on the west without any results. Bill Wernecke took over the controls as we returned to a spot where we had first tipped down and we started our search to the east. On the third sortie into the soft snow we were stopped suddenly by impact with Lewishon's snowmobile. It was completely covered by snow, and we could not see whether it was upright or over on its side.

We backed off a few yards and I organized a work party of the three Lawrences, Mike Haley, Jeff English and Sid Garrell. I told Garrell, "You stay with the Lawrences and do what they tell you. They'll show you how to use the tools. You may as well start learning about this storm right away."

He suddenly lost all of his swagger and his fright showed through on his white face. He bent over to put on his snow boots, then quickly put on his hood. "I'm ready to go," he said.

I slapped him on the shoulder. "It won't be easy," I said, "but we'll see that you get back."

The door was jammed shut by the deep snow so we used the top hatch to get out. I went first with a converter and Bandburger torch and slid down the roof into snow over my head. I melted out an area for the others and when we were all down I melted our way to the Lewishon vehicle.

We cleared off the snow and found it was on its side, the nose down at an angle of about forty degrees. We melted the snow from around it with our converters and then placed two Corning jacks under the body. The Lawrences and Garrell took care of the rear and Haley, English and I worked on the front downward end. When the jacks were placed, we raised the vehicle slowly upright. I cleared the snow and ice from the door with my converter and went inside.

The cabin was an unbelievable mess. The lights were burning very dimly so I couldn't see too much, but it appeared that seats and bunks had been ripped up and strewn about. It was icy cold inside. Harvey Lewishon was at the door and wrung my hand silently. He had a gash on his forehead and the blood had streaked down his face and dried. There were cries of anguish and calls for help from many of the company. Two girls in a seat behind the control area were sobbing hysterically.

"Get your people calmed down and put them to work straightening out this mess," I told him. "Is the intercom working?"

"All of our cabin power has failed," he said. "I'll see what I can do with the people."

He went to the two girls first and shook them. One looked up at him, still sobbing. He slapped her face. I turned away and slid into the co-pilot's seat and told George Farrell, in the pilot's place, to test the controls. The power to the wheels still worked, thank God. I took the controls then and backed a foot or two and judged there would be no trouble getting the machine out.

I returned to the work party and told Perry Lawrence to take them back to our vehicle. "Tell Bill Wernecke to wait for us at the top of the crevasse and lead us back to Jordan's machine. Tell him to go slow. Our Maser Screen doesn't work and we have no radiophone. I'll have to follow him within sight. He'll know what to do."

I returned to Lewishon's snowmobile and found the entire party up and working, with Harvey and Farrell moving among them giving instructions and encouragement. I rigged my converter, adjusted for low heat, so that it would warm the cabin and then slipped into the pilot's seat and started slowly to back out of the crevasse.

We finally reached the level crust and I stopped there, waiting for Bill Wernecke to find me and lead me on. He came out of the white wall of snow to my left and stopped a moment, then led on east. Lewishon dropped into the co-pilot's seat.

"We're all organized again," he said. "I guess we had given up, back there in the hole. We all looked square into the face of death. People aren't constructed for that sort of thing."

I pointed out the front window. "That's the face of death, right out there. Get to know it well and you'll lose your fear of it. Tell your people that, Lewishon. Don't let them panic or you'll surely be lost."

He sat silent for several minutes. "Back in the Complex," he said at last, "I was prepared to die. Now I'm going to have to prepare to live again."

It was dark when we rejoined Jordan's machine and I maneuvered ours between the two of them and facing in the opposite direction so our door was less than two feet away from that of my company. I went back aboard and sent Bill Wernecke and Fred Lawrence to Lewishon's machine to trace the power failure. I told them to let me know when they had it fixed and I crawled back into my bunk and resumed my sleep where I'd left off—but without the dream.

I was awakened in two hours by Bill Wernecke, who reported that they had found two ruptured lines due mainly to faulty design. Our three machines were under way again by 11:00 P.M. We were heading a few degrees south of east, on a base course of zero nine five, to pass over Lexington City. During the two days of radio reception, on May 17th and 18th, we had contacted two VHF stations there and we had high hopes that we might be in time to help in the rescue of more people. They had told us that more than 100 persons had got out in two of the many huge snow vehicles they had begun constructing in September after hearing the reports of Dr. Harrow, Foster Crandall from England and Hjalmer Bornstein from Norway. Five more machines were ready to go, they had said, but they had to build a new tunnel and ramp because of the ice action that had destroyed their first one.

We had speculated on machines that would hold as many as 50 persons and we had tried to get the dimensions and specifications, but the radio blackout had resumed before this information was forthcoming.

Lexington City was about 125 miles to the east and our Murphy's Brain told us we should get there in 17 days. But once again we weren't even close. We didn't arrive until June 28th, and all we got from our UHF and VHF receivers on the Lexington City frequencies was static.

I have not been able to determine to this date what was the fate of the Lexington City survivors or their vehicles built to hold 50 persons.

CHAPTER EIGHTEEN

IN THE PERIOD before Kentucky Complex all of the personality conflicts among our group had been smoothed out to a marked degree, and our experience there had added greatly to our spirit, for we had been able to help people in peril who needed desperately the very qualities we had generated.

There were no reservations in our welcome of the new-comers Chriss Lewishon, Mike Haley, Jeff English, Fritz Richter, Sid Garrell and Lily Fortune, just as there had been none with Dennis and Bettina Livingstone. But Sylvia Lawrence became upset at the quick friendship that grew up between Sam Houston and Lily Fortune and became loudly argumentative. Florence Donner found that Jack Osborne was spending too much time with Chriss Lewishon and resented it angrily. Georgia Lawrence made a play for both Jeff English and Mike Haley and brought about a bitter rivalry between the two former friends. Then Lily, bored with Sam Houston's inexperience and ineptness, switched to Jeff English and that brought on a war to the death between Lily and Georgia. Sid Garrell started petting Bettina

Livingstone and attempted to introduce her into the mysteries of sex play, and that aroused Marge. Martha Wernecke proclaimed that this was no atmosphere in which to bring up her children, and both Rufe Howard and Gabe Harrow got into it by attempting to restrain Georgia. To top it all off, an unnaturally close friendship developed between Dennis Livingstone and Tony Wernecke, and Rufe Howard told Bill Wernecke that he believed both boys should receive the Gerber Therapy as soon as possible, which aroused Bill to the point of violence.

The 125-mile trek during most of the month of June to Lexington City was one miserable, petty crisis after another, and I am frank to admit that I could find no way to deal with any of them. Marge became more and more critical and less friendly, and I felt more completely alone than I have ever felt in my life before. Day by dreary day the crises grew. By June 28th, when we were over Lexington City casting about fruitlessly for some sign of life below, it seemed that just one more tantrum by Georgia or one more screaming protest by Lily Fortune would light the fuse to blow us all apart.

Marge came up to the control area that evening and sat on the edge of the navigation table. "You've got to do something, Vic," she said. "We can't go on like this!"

"Do what?" I asked.

"Well, damn it, you're the commander of this outfit! You figure out what to do!"

"These are all adults," I said. "They know what the score is."

"They are not adults!" she exclaimed. "They're children and they need to be restrained. You took care of us all well enough back at Harrow farm."

"The situation is entirely different," I replied. "There's just nothing we can do while we're traveling."

"You'd better figure out something or we're all going to kill each other," she said.

The morning when our three vehicles resumed their Eastward course from Lexington City (we had remained over the city all night trying to make radio contact) I issued the Ten Orders that later were so severely criticized as an overreaching of my authority and attempt on my part to ape the Dictators of the Dark Centuries. I was convinced then and I am still convinced that these decrees were necessary for our survival.

Order No.1 was: "All sexual relationships of any nature whatsoever are banned for the duration of this voyage."

Order No.2: "No sleeping berth shall be occupied at any time by more than one person."

Order No.3: "All curtains separating compartments and berths are to be removed."

Order No.4: "All friendships between members of this group must remain obviously platonic."

Order No.5: "Sole authority for discipline rests in the Commander. Parents may not discipline children nor will any member of the group give orders to another or otherwise attempt to restrain the actions of another without the express consent of the Commander."

Order No.6: "There will be no disputes between group members under any circumstances of provocation."

Order No.7: "Enticement of males by females is expressly forbidden."

Order No.8: "Enticement of females by males is expressly forbidden."

Order No.9: "Violation of any of these orders under any circumstances whatsoever is punishable by death."

Order No.10: "The Commander reserves the sole right to enforce these orders and to punish violators."

I read the orders over the intercom at 8:00 A.M. on June 29 and then I had Georgia type a copy of them and post them on the control area partition.

They were received in silence. I had expected an outcry—a score of voices raised in criticism and denunciation. But the most reaction I got was a wry smile from redheaded Florence Donner standing to my left in communications.

About a half-hour later Marge came up and perched once more on the navigation desk. "You didn't have to do all that," she said in a low tone.

"I thought a lot about it, Marge. I couldn't see that halfway measures would solve anything."

"But no sex!" she exclaimed.

"That's the one order that's going to clear up this mess."

"You can't legislate against it!"

"I can drive it underground, Marge, where it won't cause any trouble. What else do you think has thrown us into a turmoil? It was bad enough when we had Georgia alone, but with those other two, Chriss and Lily, we've lost our balance completely."

"Why do you blame the girls? The men have more to do with it than any of us! That Jeff English is the real bad actor! And that nasty Sid Garrell!"

"I'm not blaming anybody. It's human nature that's to blame. It's merely that Georgia, Chriss and Lily are very obvious and very enticing females, so I've made it illegal to be enticing."

"I suppose I'm not enticing!" she exclaimed.

"You have more allure than any of them but you're not obvious about it. Let's keep this impersonal, Marge."

"You'll keep it impersonal," she said, getting up. "From now on you don't exist for me!"

The Ten Orders had two effects that were noticeable immediately. The first was a sudden end to our high spirits, as a group, and the setting in of another depression. The second was the termination of practically all of the friendly feeling I had received personally from the company.

From one moment to the next, they changed from friends to strangers—from people I liked and could trust to a group of inimical unknowns. The three exceptions were Gabe Harrow, Rufe Howard and Bill Wernecke. Even Marge was lost to me.

"I don't know whether you've done right or not," said Gabe. "Time will prove that, one way or the other. Heroic measures were called for, I'll admit that. So let's see what happens without sex."

"It wasn't my intention to keep these orders effective longer than absolutely necessary," I said. "What I had in mind, actually, was some quick and dramatic counterirritant that would shock them all out of their bickering and quarreling."

"You've certainly achieved that," said Rufe. "It's the first peaceful day we've had since Kentucky Complex. But I wouldn't keep those rules in effect too long. Otherwise you'll lose all of the good you've gained."

"I figured about a week," I said. "I don't want to force any of them to the breaking point."

CHAPTER NINETEEN

THE PALL OF DEPRESSION thickened, and by July second our company was back in its pre-St. Louis mood of deepest apathy. It was a worrisome situation to me, for I considered that I alone was responsible for it with my Ten Orders:

I needed advice badly—the kind Marge could give me—but I found it impossible to reach her. Gabe Harrow and Rufe Howard were no help, for they both told me to leave things as they were—that the Ten Orders were causing no discomfort and were largely forgotten.

A further complication, and one that caused me a great deal more concern than the mood of our company, was the increasing difficulty encountered by our two Kentucky machines in negotiating the snow in this area. The snow seemed to be much softer and the supporting crust, such as it was, down much deeper, so that most of the time we barely had clearance under our chassis. The two other snowmobiles sank deeper than we and lost all of their advantage of the larger wheels. At least once an hour one or the other of them would become mired when the snow, accumulating under the chassis, would slow them and cause the wheels to dig too deep. I thought at first that a proper use of the converters would have prevented this and I suggested it to both Bob Jordan and Harvey Lewishon over the FX. Bob assured me repeatedly that the converters were of little or no help—that the basic problem was too much weight for the crust, but there wasn't a thing we could do about weight out in the storm. Sooner or later we'd have to be sending work parties out into our violent world to get one or both of these machines free.

It came sooner rather than later. Both Kentucky machines stopped together within a half an hour, stuck fast. I called for a work party over the intercom of Perry Lawrence and his two sons, Mike Haley, Jeff English, Fritz Richter and Sid Garrell. Meanwhile Bill Wernecke, who was piloting, turned back to the two vehicles and stopped within a few feet of the first.

The mutiny developed slowly. It was no sudden flare-up of tempers kindled by the match of my work order. Their rebellion was against the storm itself in a general way, but specifically against incarceration and inaction in the snowmobile and against my Ten Orders.

It started almost undetected with a remark by Sid Garrell. He said, "The hell with this! Why should I break my neck for those monkeys?"

He had come to the forward end with helmet and snow boots, however, and I believe that then he had every intention of obeying my orders, no matter what his personal feelings were and no matter how great his resentment. However, Garrell was still scared more consciously than the rest and he couldn't hide it. I was occupied with Perry Lawrence and Sam Houston gathering our tools and other gear and I didn't hear what replies the others made to Garrell. Haley, English and Richter were close to him and talking to him, and they must have inflamed his resentment.

When I returned forward from a rear hatch with torches and jacks, I was faced with these four, lined up with their backs to the windshield, in attitudes of belligerence.

I handed a jack to Garrell and he refused to take it. "Take this," I ordered. "What's come over you?"

"We're not going out," he said.

"*We're* not going out?" I demanded. "Who's we?"

"The four of us," said Jeff English. "We've had enough of this—pushing around!"

I raised my voice, then, but I was not angry, nor did I see any seriousness in the situation. I believed I could persuade them to obey my order without making a great issue of it.

"Don't be damn fools!" I said. "Do you think I'm going to abandon those people?"

"We're not going out!" yelled English, matching my tone.

"Take this jack," I said, pushing it at him. "Stop being an ass."

I think that at that moment the entire rebellion would have ended, for English did take the jack and a look of uncertainty came over his face. But right then another factor entered the crisis.

Georgia Lawrence was on watch in communications, and she stood at the entrance to the booth, taking in the argument. I had noticed her out of the corner of my eye, but I gave her presence no particular thought. I should have. At the instant of decision, when Jeff English had taken the jack, she screamed at him, "Tell him to go to hell!"

Jeff's look of uncertainty was suddenly replaced by one of anger. He dropped the jack at my feet and yelled, "To hell with you!"

I hit out fast and hard, catching English on the jaw with my fist and knocking him into Garrell.

Georgia kept screaming, "Jump him! Mike, jump him! Kill the son of a bitch!"

Haley and Richter started for me fast and I slammed a fist into Richter's midsection, putting him out of action. But Haley had his arms around me and was wrestling me to the floor. Garrell, meanwhile, had recovered his balance and both he and English jumped me from behind. One of them hit me a glancing blow on the cheek.

Then Georgia was standing over me with the converter from the front rack pointed at my head, her finger on the release button.

Over the intercom came Marge's voice. "Drop that converter, Georgia! I'll burn you to a crisp!"

I rolled under English and Garrell out of range of the converter and managed a kick at Haley that sent him into Georgia. The melee was getting under control and I was rising to my feet when I saw Gabe Harrow, who had come plunging out of the co-pilot's seat, make a grab for Georgia's converter. Her finger was still on the release button and the blast of her converter caught Gabe full in the chest.

Georgia was screaming all the while like a maddened animal and she started once more to turn the converter toward me. I went back down to the deck fast and started to roll. Suddenly her scream was cut off, Marge had sent a narrow-angle converter blast at her from ten feet away and Georgia was suddenly dead, a small black hole through her forehead.

I grabbed the converter out of her lifeless hands. Haley and Garrell were still on the deck. English was on his feet facing me. Perry Lawrence grabbed him and started to haul

him off to the rear. Bill Wernecke was out of the pilot's seat
and he and Jack Osborne were moving toward the other two.

Rufe Howard came up to my side and we both bent over
Gabe Harrow. His chest was heaving and he was groaning
out his agony, I looked at the converter setting and saw it was
at wide-angle ten (medium-low) and I thanked God Georgia
had not known how to set it for killing. Rufe brushed away
the charred cloth of Gabe's arctics with a gentle hand, then
took a bottle from his bag and wetted a bandage, which he
placed on his chest.

Marge knelt beside me and put an arm around me. "You
all right?" she asked.

I kissed her ear. "I'm fine," I said. "Thanks for the help."

"I'm not proud of that," she said, bowing her head. There
were tears in her eyes.

"You didn't have much choice," I told her. "The girl had
gone mad."

"She was always insane," said Marge. "We should have
taken better care of her."

She looked over at Georgia's body, lying where she had
fallen, one leg curled under her and her arms stretched wide
as though she were inviting an embrace. Fred and Sam
Houston Lawrence were standing looking down at their sister, their faces expressionless. Then they leaned down together and picked her up and carried her to the seat behind
the communications booth. Sylvia Lawrence brought them a
blanket to cover her with. She shook her head at her two
sons in a meaningless gesture.

"We can take Gabe to a bunk now," said Rufe. "This
shot'll keep him asleep for hours." Rufe and I carried him.

We passed Haley, English, Richter and Garrell standing in
the galley under the guard of Perry Lawrence and Jack
Osborne. Perry was holding a converter at his side. Only
Perry and Jack looked at us as we passed.

I returned to the galley after depositing Gabe and faced our rebels. They kept their eyes cast down. All the rest of the company had their attention focused on us and I noticed particularly Lily Fortune and Chriss Lewishon, kneeling on the seat just ahead of the galley facing us. Lily's lips were wet and her eyes shone with anticipation. Chriss looked frightened.

"You four are going to have to face the consequences of your mutiny," I said. "We don't want you with us but there is no place for you to go now, so you must remain. When it is practical, you will be given a trial. For the present, you will occupy the last two seats on the left and you may not leave these seats without permission. Professor Osborne will be your guard for the present, and, if he is not satisfied in any way with your conduct, a trial will be dispensed with. Jefferson English, do you hear me?"

"Yes, sir."

I questioned the others and received the same reply. Then I took Perry Lawrence and his two sons and young Dennis Livingstone and we five went out into the storm to free the two Kentucky snowmobiles.

CHAPTER TWENTY

THE MUTINY, the death of Georgia and the serious wounding of Gabe Harrow was a sudden shocking development that was almost more than we could handle emotionally. Rufe and I concentrated on the operation and navigation of our vehicle and that removed much of the strain the others were under.

I went back to Marge, lying in her bunk, and talked to her whenever I could leave the navigating but I had little success comforting her. She was inconsolable at the tragic death of Georgia and her part in it, and she blamed herself over and over for not having taken a greater interest in the girl and her problems and for not having tried to help her. But Marge and I were close together again as a result of the crisis and all of the understanding and feeling returned.

Shortly after dark I had Chriss signal the other two machines over the FX that we were stopping and that we would let them know when to resume. I announced over the intercom that there would be a service for Georgia Lawrence.

Perry Lawrence carried the body of his daughter, wrapped in its blanket, to the front and laid it gently by the door. I read the service for the dead from my prayer book. Then I opened the door and Perry Lawrence placed the body of his daughter in the snow.

CHAPTER TWENTY-ONE

THE MONTHS OF July and August trudged by with the deadly slowness of the glaciers moving far beneath us, each day a seemingly endless procession of dull hours occupying an eternity to crawl into oblivion.

After the mishap of July second, which preceded the mutiny, we had devised a different method of travel, necessitated by the excess weight of the two Kentucky vehicles and their inability to remain on top of the snow crust. It was either that or abandon them and their fifty-two people, which was unthinkable. We went first with our snowmobile, all converters turned on, and melted out a roadway. We would do a stretch of about a mile at a time, then wait until the melted portion froze solid. The two Kentucky machines would then traverse this portion and we would proceed to melt out the next mile. It was necessary to halt after each mile and wait for them so that they could sight us accurately on their Maser Screens and keep in the roadway, for by the time the ice had frozen, the roadway was covered over and obliterated by the snow and could not be distinguished from the rest of the snowscape.

At each change of course we had to stop and wait. At each area of soft snow we had to stop and wait. We were actually under way about half of the time, but even so we managed to average some ten miles eastward on good days, which was every bit as much as we had been able to make prior to Kentucky Complex. As we came to the foothills of the Appalachians the middle of August, there were long successions of days when we would be going north or south in search of a bridge of hard snow. On other days—and far too often—we would come to absolute dead ends, where two crevasses filled with their soft snow joined at an angle, and we would have to reverse our course and spend more days hunting for a way around.

Then as we got up the gradual Western slope of the mountains we suddenly found snow with a crust that would support the two heavier vehicles without difficulty. We were able to abandon our melting-and-waiting process and proceed at good speed, for us, which was three or four miles per hour. There was nothing different to see or to feel or to be aware of in any way, yet the increased rate of our progress gave a most unexpected lift to our spirits. By the time we reached Roanoke Center, on September eighth, our company was lively and almost gay.

The one constantly worrisome situation to me, and to the others, was the unsatisfactory condition of Gabe Harrow. He had been much more badly burned than we had at first believed and he had apparently suffered serious internal injuries from the penetrating rays, which would not respond to treatment. Rufe Howard tried all of the techniques known to medicine, plus a number of new drugs that he had on hand, but Gabe continued to weaken.

On September fifth, starting at around 8:00 A.M., we had another sudden period of good radio reception and Rufe spent the seven hours it lasted making inquiries for specialists who might have discovered some new treatments for converter burns. He found only one specialist available to a UHF radio broadcaster and he was unable to suggest anything of importance.

Gabe was in great pain most of the time and Rufe gave him hourly shots of corradone derivatives to make life bearable. He remained lucid and was even cheerful at times, however, and he insisted upon getting out of his bunk at least once a day and walking up and down the aisle of our vehicle visiting with his friends. They included our four "prisoners"—Richter, English, Haley and Garrell, who were always ready to see that any slightest whim of Gabe's was satisfied immediately; in fact, they were much the same way with all of us, although perhaps not as solicitous.

The four occupied an ambiguous place in our company following the mutiny. They accepted the responsibility for what they had done. But they refused to accept the ostracism that had first been imposed. They ignored it with effective determination. They called themselves fools and worse, yet insisted that they be given a chance to atone. But it was Gabe Harrow who swung the balance in their favor more than any general relationship. Gabe started making daily visits to their prison area as soon as he was permitted to get up and he spent as much time as he was able chatting with them and setting us all an example of forgiveness. Gabe was making no grandstand play about it; he was merely following a deeply formed impulse to be kindly.

I modified the restrictions on our prisoners at the end of the first week. I went back to them and I told them that they no longer would be required to confine themselves to their four seats and that their guard would be removed. I warned them that they were still subject to trial for the mutiny, and that any breach of discipline or good manners would be summarily dealt with.

All four of them thanked me, with restraint, and that was the end of that. Later on that evening I rescinded seven of the Ten Orders. I retained Order No.5—sole authority for discipline, etc.—Order No.6, banning disputes, and Order No. 10, reserving for myself the sole right of enforcement.

The compartment curtains went back up and anyone could entice anyone else—only I hoped they wouldn't. I didn't have much faith that Lily Fortune would submerge her impulses much longer or that she wouldn't find plenty of co-operation among our younger members, but I felt I had to take a chance that these activities would not disrupt our lives, as they had when she had first joined our group and collided head on with the rivalry of Georgia. Chriss Lewishon I didn't worry about. There had been nothing harmful about her friendship with Jack Osborne; it had been merely that the general atmosphere was inflammable and that Florence Donner had chosen to react in her redheaded way. Chriss was not a Lily Fortune.

The radio-reception period of September fifth, aside from our disappointment about obtaining help for Gabe Harrow, brought us the best news we had received since the previous September. We received reports from two Equatorial stations, one at Africa East at Kenya Complex, where the temperature was 37 degrees Fahrenheit and it was raining heavily, and the second from the island of Ceylon, where the temperature was 39 degrees, with milder rain. The wind at both places was a meager 40 miles per hour.

I announced this heartening news to our company over the intercom and a yell went up that drowned out the roar of the storm. Chriss Lewishon, on duty in communications in Georgia's place, passed the news on to the two Kentucky vehicles and there was much brave talk over the FX phones for the next hour.

At this time of our general elation we were talking to a score of stations along the Atlantic coast from Florida Complex to York Area and a dozen more throughout the rest of the world. We logged 33 VHF and UHF broadcasters in all, but there was no station broadcasting from Roanoke Center. Finally we were informed by a station at Virginia Complex, some 130 miles to the north and east, that the last Roanoke Center station had gone off the air in May. We had a long talk with various people at this Virginia station and they were even more interested in us and our long trek from Kansas than in giving us information about themselves. They told us that several thousands of their survivors had gone to the ocean in snow vehicles that had been plying regularly between Virginia and Norfolk Complexes. However, ice movement and destruction had forced the abandonment of Norfolk and the refugee ships were coming no farther North than Charleston Complex. Those left in Virginia Complex were living safely and relatively comfortably far underground. They had several snow vehicles with them and planned eventually to start South in them and seek to embark on a ship for the Equator.

Both Bill Wernecke and I tried to persuade them to leave their underground caves immediately and try to put their own ship into commission at Norfolk, as we planned to do. We warned them that the longer they delayed the less chance they would have of digging or melting their way to the top of the snow, but they refused to accept our advice.

We raised one station at Norfolk Complex, apparently the last still operating. I talked to Ludlow Fisher, leader of sixty-odd survivors, the last, he thought, in the Complex. He told me they were doing the final work on an 120-foot powerboat to take them all South. He asked me immediately how many there were in our party and when I told him 75, he groaned with disappointment. "We have room for ten or a dozen in our boat but no more than that," he said. "I was hoping you all could come along with us."

"We couldn't get there for another six or eight weeks," I said. "We're only at Roanoke now."

He was silent for several minutes. "You people know any-thing about boats?" he asked.

I told him that we did, that we had an engineer and a doctor with us who had sailed extensively and that I had had the usual Academy training and knew about construction, power and operation of various types of vessels.

"You better go to the Navy Yard," he said. "There are hundreds of boats there you could put into commission. They kept the whole area clear of ice up until last month, so you'll find nothing but soft snow over the place. You got plenty of converters and tools?"

"Enough," I replied. "Can you tell me about other condi-tions that would affect us?"

"The bay and the harbor are frozen over," he said. "The ice extends about a mile off-shore in the Atlantic and it's precarious going. The farther out you get, the worse the ice is. Huge cakes are piled up on end, and the wind and snow lash you unmercifully. The waves break at the edge of the ice and send frozen spray a mile in when the gusts of wind shift around. You can't drag a boat over the ice. You've got to melt a channel with converters. Now I'll tell you how to do that. You—"

It was 3:10 P.M. of September fifth, and that was the sudden end of the seven-hour period of radio reception.

I have not to this date found Ludlow Fisher and his party of sixty-odd in the RSA and so I've never found out how he would have melted a channel through the ice at Norfolk.

CHAPTER TWENTY-TWO

SEVENTY MILES EAST of Roanoke we encountered so many snow-filled crevasses that an entire week of laborious seeking for ways around gave us a total eastward progress daily of only a few miles.

However, the temperature moderated to between zero and two degrees above zero and the wind velocity reduced to 60 to 80 miles per hour, so we had that much to be thankful for. Then suddenly tragedy struck once more.

On September 23rd, at 9:15 P.M., shortly after we had stopped at the end of a mile stretch of ice-road we had just completed, we received one short SOS over the FX phone from the Lewishon vehicle. Then silence. We tried for several minutes to raise them by phone and short wave but there was no response.

I had notified Bob Jordan and he gave me the last position of Lewishon's machine as best he could estimate, but he said he had no exact idea how far behind him Lewishon had been traveling. He said he had not been in touch with him for nearly an hour and had presumed that he was close behind and proceeding normally.

The SOS had been particularly uninformative. It was a girl's voice and she had said, "SOS Lewishon vehicle. We're in trouble." That was all. Either the FX had gone dead at that point before she could say more or some other dire emergency had prevented further speech.

We went back over the ice-road around Jordan's machine and started searching, making a series of circles until we would come to a crevasse, then searching that every ten feet or so. We found two crevasses in the next four hours and we searched each for more than a mile, but we found no trace of the Lewishon machine. Then we came to a third crevasse close to our former course. We went sliding into it and down some fifty feet before we came to a halt. We were partly over on our side and in a precarious situation, for it seemed that at any moment we would begin to slide down again and not stop until we hit bottom. Bottom could have been anywhere from 100 to 500 feet down.

Bill Wernecke, Perry Lawrence and his two sons, Sid Garrell and I climbed out of the roof hatch with torches, jacks and converters and went to work. Garrell had insisted upon coming with us and I saw no reason why he should not.

We first melted a huge shelf back into the walls of the crevasse so that our machine could sit level and not slide further down. It came to rest on its side and we eased it slowly upright with jacks. Then we started melting a ramp by which we could climb out.

Chriss Lewishon and Florence Donner, meanwhile, kept in touch with Bob Jordan and both machines kept constantly calling the Lewishon machine on all the different wave lengths and FX. At some time after 3:00 A.M. we finally returned to the top of the crust with the aid of our thrust engine. There was still no word from Lewishon.

We sat up on the edge of the steep crevasse while I tried to decide what to do next. I had a strong feeling that Lewishon's machine had gone into this crevasse and that it was resting somewhere on the bottom, but it did not seem to me that I could risk the lives of our company by taking our machine back down into this great fissure.

Sid Garrell came up to the navigation desk and asked me formally whether he could speak to me.

"Sure. Go ahead, Sid."

"I could get down to the bottom of that crevasse with a converter," he said. "I could dig my way through it and I could find that other machine—if it's down there."

"You could die trying, too," I said.

"It's the only way!" he exclaimed. "You can tie a rope around me and haul me out if I get into trouble. There are twenty-six people in that machine," he went on. "It's my one life against theirs. You couldn't ask for a better gamble."

"Okay," I said. "Check your arctics and make sure the heater is charged."

Perry Lawrence, Bill Wernecke and I went back into the storm with Garrell, Perry carrying a coil of drinal-cord that had a tensile strength of several tons. One end was tied around Garrell's shoulders and under his arms. He carried a converter and torch and a Corning jack strapped to his back.

Garrell started down into the crevasse, his converter melting out a path down the ramp we had used to climb out. Wernecke played out the line at the edge of the decline and Perry unwound it as Garrell descended. We had set up three signals on the rope. Three tugs meant he had found the snowmobile. Four tugs meant we were to pull him up. Two tugs would tell us he was in trouble.

We had marked the line for every fifty feet. In a little under an hour Perry had played out 600 feet of line and Garrell was still going. He had slowed down considerably and we judged that he had reached the bottom of the crevasse and was exploring along its length. At 650 feet there were three tugs on the rope. He had found the snowmobile. Another twenty-five feet of rope was pulled out, then there were four tugs and we started to haul it in. We were down to 300 feet of line when it suddenly became stuck fast. The three of us pulled as hard as we could but we couldn't budge it.

We waited for a moment for some signal on the line but none came.

"The snow has collapsed on him," yelled Bill Wernecke in my ear, over the howl of the wind.

"Come on!" I bellowed at him, motioning toward the snowmobile.

We played out the line to our vehicle and I looped and tied it around a bar across the chassis. I yelled at Bill Wernecke to get inside and back up slowly. Then Perry and I returned to the edge of the crevasse to guide the line.

It pulled taut for a moment, then jerked upward suddenly and moved easily after that. In a few minutes Sid Garrell came into sight. Perry Lawrence ran to stop the snowmobile and I held up the boy's limp body and walked with him. I determined that he still had a pulse before the machine came to a stop.

I carried Garrell into the vehicle and Rufe Howard went to work on him immediately with an oxygen inhalator and also blowing his own breath into his lungs. He had him breathing more or less normally within five minutes and shortly afterwards Garrell opened his eyes and fixed them on me. Finally recognition came into them and he shook his head slowly.

"They were all dead," he said.

Then he closed his eyes and seemed to go to sleep.

For long afterwards I was haunted by a feeling of guilt. Harvey Lewishon should have remained in Kentucky Complex with his Chriss.

CHAPTER TWENTY-THREE

SID GARRELL LIVED, although he still had a short bout of pneumonia to go through before he was back to normal, and Gabe Harrow began unaccountably to improve. On November 17th at 9:30 A.M. we arrived over dead and abandoned Norfolk Complex, the goal we had set for ourselves more than a year before, when we had first unloaded the crated parts of our snowmobile from the Gar-Ring at Harrow farm.

I cannot begin to describe the feelings we had as the end of our frightful voyage through the storm drew to a close. We thanked God with all the sincerity and whole feeling of children.

It was as nothing to us then that we yet faced the almost impossible tasks of finding a boat, putting it into commission, getting it out into the ocean and then sailing it through the violent tempest to the South. We felt that if we would survive the snow we could survive anything.

There was something very incongruous about this, because not on November 17th nor the next day were we different in any way. It was the same violent, howling wind—still between 60 and 80 miles per hour—the same solid, swirling wall of snow, the same deadly cold, and the same slow and endless progress. You still could not see anything but the storm, and you could not feel anything or hear anything but its bluster and uproar.

The Norfolk Complex radio station of Ludlow Fisher was silent.

I had not been able to talk to Fisher long enough to find out how to get down to the Complex and to the Navy Yard—whether there were any buildings intact or ramps still usable. We had learned in our conversations with Virginia Complex that there had been two ramps at one time, but both had been abandoned when the port became unusable.

I pondered long over this problem before one possible solution occurred to me. Then I continued toward the ocean, for somewhere out in that direction the snow would come to an end and the ice and water would begin. But I was fully aware that this was a dangerous procedure also, because it was quite possible that the end of the deep snow would be a precipice perhaps a thousand feet high, and that if we should fall off it or slide down it out of control, we would surely be killed.

I told Bob Jordan to explore various drifts and hummocks in the area over the Complex to see if a building was still standing and that I would be back for him within twenty-four hours, we went North toward the Navy Yard and the sea. After several hours we came to a great declivity, the edge of which extended in a Northerly direction, I plotted our position as accurately as possible with the Dace Recorder and Haverwood Navigator and it appeared that this was at the edge of the Navy Yard area. We explored the full extent of this snow-cliff to the north—a distance of four miles—and followed it around to the West for a mile. I plotted the cliff on a Complex map and found that it did coincide with the boundary of the Navy Yard and that there could be no doubt this sunken area of soft snow was that described to us by Ludlow Fisher.

We turned north again then and continued toward the open sea, proceeding at less than a mile an hour. Visibility was never more than ten feet. I had the frightening feeling that at any moment we would begin to plunge downward, and I turned on our forward converters and adjusted the angles so that the two blasts would meet some twenty feet ahead of us. Thus there was a small clear area directly in front of our machine that would enable us to see any sudden drop in time to stop.

Bill Wernecke piloted and I navigated. Gabe Harrow, his health seemingly restored, sat next to Bill and acted as look-out. Florence Donner was in communications and was in constant touch with Bob Jordan over FX.

The edge of the deep snow was an anticlimax. We came suddenly to a vertical cliff and before Bill Wernecke could stop the snowmobile we started to slide downward, for a horrible moment I thought that we were going to plunge hundreds of feet to the bottom and I gripped the sides of my seat. Less than ten feet down we came to a soft stop, buried in snow up to our roof.

We turned on our converters and melted ourselves into the clear. We were in a huge snow-slide with the surface at an angle of 30 or 35 degrees. There had been a cliff there once but apparently it had collapsed. The snow was very soft and we melted our way straight down for a hundred feet, then moved slowly forward for another fifty feet. We started melting again and got down fifty feet more. By this time the water from our melting had formed ice all around us and under us and we were able to burn out a tunnel and proceed down a grade of ten or twelve per cent. We came to solid ice underneath the top snow in another three hundred feet and built ourselves a huge tunnel through it and in a direction parallel to the upper cliff. Something under a mile farther along we came into the open again, resting on several feet of snow and ice particles and buffeted by the most violent wind we had yet encountered. This violence came from explosive gusts that hit us from every direction rather than the wind velocity itself, for the maximum gust we measured on our gauge was 84 miles per hour.

As we came to a stop on the hard surface we were battered by a hail of ice that bounced off our cabin like handfuls of rocks thrown by a malicious giant. The noise was deafening, and I imagined that this is how it must have been under bombardment in one of the old-fashioned wars of our unenlightened ancestors.

We knew that not very far out was the surging, churning ocean but we could not see it nor could we hear it over the roar of the wind and the battering of the ice. It seemed to me that getting a boat through this gale and over this ice out into the water was going to be a task completely beyond the strength of mere men. But then I remembered Ludlow Fisher and his confident account of what they were doing and what they were going to do and I lost some of my pessimism.

We continued on North for a half a mile and were stopped suddenly by huge ice cakes jutting from below, forming a great jagged wall. We turned to our left and ran parallel to this barrier for two and a half miles, which brought us to the entrance to Hampton Roads. We turned left again, heading southwest into the bay and came to an area of relatively soft snow that would not support the weight of our vehicle. We used our converters and determined that we could melt our way through it, for we were resting on solid ice and we did not sink farther down from the melting. We could not see to the top of the snow but we guessed from its consistency that it was no more than 200 feet deep, perhaps even less.

It was getting dark by then so we retraced our course slowly and carefully back to the tunnel through the ice and climbed up to the top of the deep snow over Norfolk Complex. We spent the night stopped there beside the snowmobile of Bob Jordan and company.

Bob and Libby came over to our machine to visit and Bob reported that he had found no buildings or evidence of ramps or other means to get down to the Complex. I told him of our explorations and said that at first light in the morning we would return together to Hampton Roads and attempt to approach the Navy Yard on the same courses the ships had once used.

The next morning, November 18th, we retraced our course north to the edge of the deep snow, thence down to the ice barrier and northwest to the Hampton Roads entrance, with Bob Jordan's machine close behind us. We started to work our way into the harbor by melting through the 200-foot snow with our converters. First we melted down to the bottom ice, then constructed a tunnel straight in. We had to build side-tunnels as we went for the water to run off, and we cut holes through the six-foot ice to the bay underneath, which took care of the tremendous floods of water from our melting. With the two snowmobiles working together on this—ours in front shaping the tunnel and Bob Jordan's behind us putting on the finishing touches and keeping the water from freezing so it could flow off—we were able to proceed at some 1,000 feet an hour. It was eleven miles from Hampton Roads entrance to the Navy Yard and it took us a little over four days to reach our goal.

We encountered a most startling and frightening phenomena on the ice that covered the bay and it took us some time to realize its significance. There was a constant sound of groaning and cracking which seemed to come from all around us, as though we were in the midst of tremendous activity in the ice itself. Bill Wernecke suggested that this was caused by actual movement of the ice due to tides and possibly glacial pressure. This view was supported by Jack Osborne, who had had similar experiences in areas of Arctic ice during an expedition in his youth.

"We're going to have to melt out a channel to get a boat through it," I said. "What happens then?"

Osborne shook his head in doubt. "Maybe we can keep it open with converters," he said. "Ordinarily the tendency would be for the channel to close up. We'll just have to try it out and see what forces are at work in this bay."

At the end of the tunnel at the Navy Yard we came to a huge concrete dock and on it was a great metal warehouse. One end of the roof had caved in from the weight of the snow but more than half of it was intact. We melted the snow and ice from around one of the large double doors and opened it. It was filled with crates of supplies of various sorts for ships and we set Richter, Haley, Sam Houston Lawrence and English to work sorting out the crates and listing their contents. Then Bill Wernecke, Rufe Howard, Perry Lawrence, Bob Jordan, two others from his machine and I armed ourselves with converters and started hunting for a suitable boat.

We found four harbor launches at the shoreward end of the dock, frozen in the ice, but all were too small. We melted a tunnel to the next pier some 50 yards to our left and we found several more launches and a tug in the ice.

We visited three more piers and went into the bilges of seven boats before we gave up finding a usable vessel that had been left in the water.

During our absence Gabe Harrow had put the rest of the company to work enlarging our tunnel and building a ramp to the end of the dock so we could explore the Navy Yard with our snowmobile. When we told him of our experiences with the boats frozen in the ice, he suggested we hunt for dry docks and shipbuilding installations where we might find boats out of the water.

Bill Wernecke, Rufe Howard and I had discussed this possibility, so the following day we took the snowmobile and began our search for the shipbuilding area of the Yard. We took a party of a dozen, leaving the rest behind in the other snowmobile and in the warehouse.

The part of the Navy Yard where we had stopped was at the juncture of the Elizabeth River and the Western Branch and seemed to contain the supply docks. We looked on our Complex map and found what appeared to be a huge basin just behind the neck of land we were on and we considered that this would be a likely place to find ship construction.

We took the entire day to tunnel our way across the two miles to the basin. The first discovery that gave us new hope was a large metal shed, still uncollapsed, which contained prefabricated pilothouses for small harbor vessels.

Since we were back under the snow as we had been at Harrow farm, our days and our nights had ceased to be distinguishable, so we continued to melt our way forward and to explore until we felt like sleeping. We finally called a halt at 11:00 P.M., without having found anything else of interest outside of an empty graving dock, and we turned in.

Then on the next day, November 25th, which shall always remain in my memory as a day of good fortune, we came upon the famous yacht *Maecenas* resting in its blanket of snow in dry-dock.

The *Maecenas,* as most of you probably know, had been the State Yacht of both Presidents Evelyn Shaw and Martin Vollmer, and had figured prominently in the accusations against Mrs. Shaw that led to her impeachment. Gamberelli had refused to use it for that reason, although everyone who knew him well was aware that the gesture was not sincere and was made only for its publicity value. The ship had been given to the Navy, which had been responsible for it anyway, and it was not heard of again by the public.

The *Maecenas* was 175 feet long, of Lomax alloy and permanium construction throughout and was equipped with Courtney stabilizers that enabled her to keep a fairly even keel in anything short of a hurricane. She was powered by two Nobel reactors and heat-differential jets that gave her a speed limited only by the amount of pounding the passengers wanted to take. Her plates were inch-thick Lomax, so the pounding would not have harmed her.

We all fell in love with her the minute we saw her. We made up our minds immediately that this was the ship that would take us south, out of the storm.

CHAPTER TWENTY-FOUR

WITH GREAT CARE and low heat we cleared the snow from the *Maecenas*, forming a giant dome of ice over the ship so that she rested in the center of a glistening cavern. We rigged Bandburger torches around the walls of the cavern and it was as light as a sunlit day. Bill Wernecke, Rufe Howard and I went over her from stem to stern and found only one major defect. She had two badly bent plates near the bow on the starboard side just under the water line and it appeared to us that she had forcefully rammed some underwater piling or other obstruction.

There was one bent frame inside the hull but the damage had not caused a leak so far as we could determine. Certainly it had not weakened her in any crucial way, for her Lomax metal frames and plates would have been able to withstand many times that damage before giving way. We found several Lomax plates at the bottom of the dry-dock, apparently brought there to repair the damage. Bill Wernecke cut out the old plates with a converter and straightened the frame under heat. He then welded in two new plates and that was that an hour's not very difficult work for an expert.

Bob Jordan meanwhile had called for his snowmobile to join us at the dry-dock and we put our entire company to work cleaning up the interior of the *Maecenas*. There was a fine layer of dust over everything—obviously accumulated before the storm. We discovered that the interior fittings and furnishings had deteriorated to an alarming degree. The more we dug into her the more we found wrong with her—all minor so far as her sea qualities were concerned, but troublesome nevertheless. A lot of her plumbing wouldn't work, much of the electric wiring had been corroded away and we discovered that her bridge controls and many of the automatic and electronic devices there were permanently out of commission.

We combed through the list of supplies we had found on the first pier and determined that we would be able to replace the wiring and most of the plumbing. We sent one snowmobile back for this material and started dismantling the other—our original Rance Goodrich vehicle—and installing the navigation devices, the intercom and all of the communications receivers and broadcasters on the ship. We took out the cabin linings and furnishings and rebuilt much of the ship's interior. With all forty-eight persons doing the work, at least half of whom had developed some mechanical skills during the various emergencies of our long voyage, we had the *Maecenas* in passable condition in a week.

We all had started living aboard her during the refurbishing and by the time the work was finished we were quite comfortably installed, with a great deal more room for each than we had had in our snow vehicles.

I think most of us felt saddened by the cannibalizing of our snowmobiles. They had meant our safety and our hope of escape for some eight months and we could not pull them apart and destroy their usefulness without regrets.

A large section of our ice-dome caved in on the second day of work and tons of snow covered the stern of our ship and most of the dry-dock. Very fortunately the cave-in occurred while we were all at lunch in the main cabin and there was no one on the deck or dry-dock. If there had been they surely would have been killed.

Gabe Harrow, although unable to sustain any physical exertion, gave tremendous moral support to our efforts and our company and became a sort of father-confessor to many of us. Both he and Rufe Howard shared this role to a certain extent, for Rufe as our physician was trusted and even revered.

I had long hours of discussion with Bill Wernecke, Rufe Howard, Jack Osborne and Bob Jordan on the best means of getting our ship out to the ocean. For a long time I doubted that it could be done at all and I was bitterly depressed as I considered that our entire company had encountered a final frustration that made our months of voyaging and struggling through the storm all come to naught. Both Bill Wernecke and Rufe Howard refused to be daunted by the enormity of the task, and Bill especially spent hours reviewing the various means by which we could accomplish it, belittling my fears and my arguments.

Our final decision was that we would leave the *Maecenas* in the dry-dock, which was a small floating dock for handling repairs on harbor craft, and attempt to move ship and dock together through the 14 or 15 miles of ice to the ocean. We had examined the hull of the dry-dock and had found it badly twisted and sprung by the ice, but there were no leaks in it that could not be handled by the pumps. These pumps were in good condition, so the idea appealed to us. But if at any time this proved impractical, we could always sink the dock in the bay and move the ship alone under its own power.

The advantages of keeping the dock as long as possible were obvious to us. For in the event of any sudden ice move-ment when we began to open up our channel, then the dock would be crushed and not our ship. The groaning and working of the ice on the bay had given us warning that we could not trust it to behave to our wishes.

On December second, shortly before noon, we started to melt the ice around the dry-dock and break it loose. We had rigged our thrust engine at the stern with a Lomax tube fashioned by Bill Wernecke at the business end, which could be lowered under water, to act as a water-jet. This would give us all the power we could possibly use for propulsion.

We used four converters for the job of floating the dry-dock. Perry Lawrence was stationed with a converter at the bow. Fred and Sam Houston at each side, and Mike Haley at the stern. In a very few minutes the dock was afloat. The deck of the *Maecenas* was crowded by our company and they sent up a loud cheer that bounced deafeningly off the ice-dome as they felt the floating movement.

Bill Wernecke lowered the thrust-engine tube into the water and turned on the power. Our four converters were moved to the bow and we began to melt out our channel and the tunnel through which we would pass.

We had folded down the short mast of the *Maecenas* and the total clearance we needed was 28 feet, which was more than twice the height we had needed for the snowmobiles. The dry-dock was 30 feet wide, so we made our tunnel two feet wider than that. The one thing we did not have to bother about was disposal of the water from the melting, so we were able to proceed at a fair rate. We found we could make some 200 to 300 feet per hour safely. This gave plenty of time for the ice on the roof and sides of our tunnel to form solidly enough to support the structure while we passed.

This worked out to 16 days for the 15 miles to the ocean, barring major mishaps.

We broke in four converter crews for the work and each crew worked four hours—four hours on and twelve off. Bill Wernecke, Perry Lawrence and I drilled our converter operators carefully and one of the three of us was always present to oversee the tunnel building. We were determined that we would have no more mishaps if our care and knowledge could prevent them.

On December seventh, a large section of tunnel behind us—probably several hundred feet of it—collapsed with a roar and threw a scare into us that redoubled our caution.

Life on board the *Maecenas* settled into the normal and traditional shipboard routine, with all members of the company assigned to divisions, duties and watches. It was very much different from our snowmobile living, for we not only had plenty of room but we found plenty of work to do, as there always is aboard a ship.

Marge and Jack Osborne resumed their daily school as soon as we got the tunnel and channel building under way and their classes were enlarged to more than a score by teenagers from the Jordan group. Martha Wernecke and Libby Jordan set up classes for Bridge instruction and got nearly the whole Jordan group playing the game before we were halfway to the ocean. Libby had taught several of these during the snowmobile trek and some excellent players came out of this company.

A Masters' Point tournament was started within the first week and ran in three sections during the day and night to accommodate those on the various watches.

Sylvia Lawrence took over the galley and invented some wondrous concoctions of food concentrates. Fritz Richter, Lily Fortune, and several talented youngsters from the Jordan group organized a theatrical company and staged one Wendover classic and a bad Fourchet comedy in the salon before we were out of our tunnel.

We had had no problems with Lily Fortune since the death of Georgia, and I had ceased my concern for her and her libido. Whatever she was doing she did in private and without disrupting the lives of the rest of us.

On December 12th, Rufe Howard came to me in my cabin and told me that Lily was pregnant.

"How far along?" I asked him.

"Three months. She was very coy about naming her collaborator but it appears to me to be Jeff English. She wouldn't say yes definitely, but she wouldn't deny it either."

"They'll have to get married," I said. "As captain of a ship, now, I can perform a ceremony without violating any of the traditions."

"You'll have to convince Jeff English," he said. "I've already talked to him and he's not in favor of it. In the first place, he doubts seriously that it's his child. He thinks it could just as easily be Mike Haley's or that of any of several of the Jordan group. He admits he's had occasional relations with Lily but he insists he was one of many."

"Where could they have had these relations?" I asked. "Three months ago we were in the snowmobile. There was nothing going on there."

"There was," said Rufe. "In your innocence you would not have noticed it, of course. Lily would get into Mike's bunk or Jeff's or Sid Garrell's, close the curtains and wait until her lover arrived. She would make sure that you or Marge or several others wouldn't see her, but she didn't care if I did."

"Well, what do we do?" I asked. "Issue a decree that Jeff English shall marry her or find her another husband?"

"Not Jeff English," he said. "Find her somebody of her own class. She and Jeff have nothing in common but sex and they're tired of that between them already."

"But who'd marry a pregnant girl?" I asked.

"Any of those young stags in the Jordan group who've slept with her," he said. "Let me find one."

"You do that," I said. "That baby has some rights."

CHAPTER TWENTY-FIVE

ON DECEMBER 13TH, two-thirds of the way to the ocean, the long channel we had left with our passage down the center of the bay began to close up shortly after 5:00 P.M. We did not have a lookout astern and we were not aware of our peril until, with frightening suddenness, the walls of the channel closed in on the hull of our dry deck and began to grind and crush the plates with loud crackings and reports of rended metal. At the same time the tunnel behind us collapsed with a whoosh and a slam and it seemed to be a matter of seconds before the roof immediately overhead would fall in on us.

Bill Wernecke was in charge of the converter crew when this crisis came upon us and he ordered converters turned upon the ice at the sides of the deck immediately to relieve the pressure and overhead as well to strengthen the roof.

The loud and ominous sound of the grinding brought most of the company to the deck. I ran to the bridge and get on the intercom, ordering them to get below and calling out the other converter crews on the double with all our converters. We had a total of eleven converters and I spaced the seven additional around the deck on both sides and told the operators they were to keep the ice back and the roof intact at all costs. Then I ran down to the dock and found Bill Wernecke sweating ever the controls of the pumps.

"We're losing our dock!" he exclaimed. "The pumps can't take care of the water. It's pouring in on both sides of the hull."

"Get the converter crew back on the boat," I said. "Let the dock sink!"

Bill got his crew up on the deck of the *Maecenas* and I took a last look around to make certain there were no lines or other gear that would foul us up when the deck sank. I was just starting up the ladder to the bow when there was another great whooshing sound and a huge section of the roof of our tunnel, with its hundreds of tons of snow, came crashing down on the stern of our ship. The dry-dock and the ship gave a great shudder and I was knocked off the ladder to the metal plates.

I must have been dazed for several minutes. When I became conscious of what I was doing, I was halfway up the ladder, scrambling as fast as my legs and arms could take me, and cursing under my breath.

Everything behind the ship's bridge was obliterated by the great mass of snow. As I stood looking horrified at it for a moment, there was movement under it and Bill Wernecke came crawling out, the side of his face laid bare and bleeding profusely. He had a converter in his hand and he shook himself, then whirled and blasted at the snow with full heat. There was a huge hole through it in an instant and water came cascading onto the deck.

I mobilized five others of the converter crews and grabbed a sixth converter from the hands of a dazed youth of the Jordan group and we started to melt away the snow from the deck and also to form a new roof. We worked frantically to repair the damage and get the snow off the ship, but we had to work carefully also because there were at least five men buried at the stern, and perhaps many more. I had not had time to check whether my order to clear the decks had been obeyed. There had still been a dozen or more men and women on the deck when I had assigned the converter crews before climbing down to the dock, although most of them had seemed to be on their way below.

It took us 20 minutes to get the snow melted down to expose the bodies of the victims. Rufe Howard was on hand at my side and as soon as the first body was uncovered he jumped into the slush and water and picked him up. It was Fritz Richter and there was no sign of a pulse. The next we found was Sam Houston Lawrence and a little further along his brother Fred, both dead.

There were eleven dead in all in this disaster of the snow and ice. There were two other converter crewmen from the Jordan group—Sylvester Gross and Carl Addams—and the rest were those who had not gone below quickly enough in response to my order. They were Alice Wernecke, Dennis and Bettina Livingstone, Jerry Grant and James Willicombe of the Jordan party and lastly, Lily Fortune. The body of Lily was lying across that of young Willicombe as though the last act of her life had been to embrace a boy of her choice.

We could take no time out to mourn our dead. The dry-dock was completely awash by this time with the water rising on our hull. The channel had continued to close and the ice had crushed in the sides of the dock so that they were in danger of fouling our bottom and sides.

I got converter crews on each side melting out the ice and the protruding metal of the dock. Bill Wernecke and I then went to the bow and started to extend our channel and our tunnel away from this unlucky spot.

A few minutes later the dry-dock lost all of its buoyancy and sank with a rush and we were afloat for the first time. We bounced about a bit as a result of the turbulence from the sinking dock and our sides bumped hard against the ice, then all was still and calm as a summer's lake, with nothing to remind us of our tragedy except the eleven bodies lying in a row on the afterdeck.

I went to the bridge and turned on both engines slow ahead and we began to move once more to the ocean.

CHAPTER TWENTY-SIX

WE HELD SERVICES on December 13th at 11:00 P.M. on the afterdeck of the *Maecenas* for our eleven dead.

Their bodies lay in a semicircle around the stern, each sewn into a white blanket and with a bar of lead ballast tied to the feet. I read the Order for the Burial of the Dead from my prayer book—"Unto Almighty God we commend the souls of our brothers and sisters departed, and we commit their bodies to the deep—" and after a short prayer Gabe Harrow and Rufe Howard slid the bodies into the channel.

I had wanted to say something more about these eleven, mentioning each by name and telling about their fortitude in the long voyage through the storm, but I found that I could not. Their sudden deaths under the snow when we had been so near to our goal after our timeless struggle were too overwhelmingly sad. The words would not come—only tears.

Perry and Sylvia Lawrence stood at my side, completely crushed by the final tragedy that had deprived them of the last of their children. The two of them suddenly seemed to grow old and tired and they stood with their heads bent low, Perry holding Sylvia's hand by his side.

I stayed up all that night helping to direct the tunnel and channel building, often using a converter myself, checking on our course and position. I had no desire for sleep and Marge felt the same way. She spent the night on the bridge and we talked for many long hours while I wasn't working.

We both watched Bill Wernecke, a great white patch on the side of his face, drive himself through the night with energy that seemed superhuman. Martha came to him several times and pleaded with him to rest but he would not hear of it. It seemed that he now looked upon the snow and the ice as personal enemies that had deprived him of his daughter— that he was bent upon battling these hostile elements in hand-to-hand combat as long as he was able to stand up.

That night, from midnight to 8:00 A.M. we progressed more than 2,500 feet with our extra converters and under the driving energy of Bill Wernecke. The clearance necessary for our boat without the dry-dock under it was only eighteen feet and our channel needed to be no more than 22 feet wide, so we had much less ice and snow to melt away. We kept all of our eleven converters working most of the time from then on. We felt that only by our determination and our labor could we thwart the hateful snow and the malevolent ice.

We asked no quarter and we gave no quarter. We worked and we fought, and on December 17th at 10:25 A.M. we emerged from under the snow into the storm.

I think we had all forgotten about the wind and the snow. I know I had, and I was surprised and shaken by the sudden violence that descended upon us when we came once more into the elements. Our small ship heeled and plunged alarmingly and was thrown violently against the ice. I didn't see how our plates could stand this pounding if we could not devise some means immediately to alleviate it.

My first thought was that a wider channel that would give us room to use our power and maneuver would end the pounding and I rushed down to Bill Wernecke in the bow and got our converter crews busy on both sides. With no roof to worry about and no careful construction needed, we were able to turn our converters on full blast and in minutes we had an area a hundred yards wide. I had returned to the bridge, and I swung the bow into the wind and put on enough power so that we held relatively steady.

We continued our wide-channel melting and I maneuvered the *Maecenas* on the various headings to meet the gusts and to keep her from pounding or capsizing. We bounced so much that it was extremely difficult for the converter men and we finally had to lash five of them to the railing forward so they could work. We had to change our crews every hour, for we found quickly that that was the limit of endurance out in the wind and the snow and the flying ice crystals that hit you like bullets.

Bill Wernecke was driven to the cabin to rest after a couple of hours of it and I spelled him on the forward deck, turning over the conn to Rufe Howard. We had to use every able-bodied male of our company on the converter relay and even Gabe Harrow and Sid Garrell, just recovering from his bout with pneumonia, took a hand. We kept this up for forty hours, resting and sleeping when we could, eating now and then and laboring to the limit of our endurance.

At least half of our company was seasick but we couldn't let that stop us, for these last interminable miles through the ice at the edge of the ocean were the most critical of all.

On December 19th at 7:40 A.M., we melted the last foot of our channel. The ice at the edge of the ocean had piled up fifty feet and more and the bombardment of the ice spray was constant. The last ten minutes we sat out there blasting the barrier, with the huge waves beginning to break in on us through the opening we had made, were a perilous eternity. It was impossible that any craft such as ours could live through such utter turbulence and I felt our small ship shudder and twist under my feet as though it were in the throes of death.

Rufe Howard and I were on the bridge together, holding on to stanchions to keep from being thrown against the bulkheads. His face was as white as the snow-wall beyond the windscreen and I am certain mine must have been too. I know that I was as frightened as I have ever been, for the balance between life and death was so fine that any slightest mishap, any momentary hesitation in our power output or failure to meet the next blast of wind from the right angle or miscalculation of the channel which we could not see except very vaguely through our Maser Screen, would have meant the end of us. There would have been no appeal, no second chance.

Bill Wernecke was back down on the heaving forward deck with an FX phone strapped to his head, a converter in his hand blasting far out into the storm. Suddenly his voice came over the loud speaker on the bridge, and the three words that he yelled were the most welcome I have ever heard in my life.

"All clear ahead!"

I turned on three-quarters power on both engines, swung the nose around to the center of the channel, and in two minutes we were out into the Atlantic Ocean.

It was a tempestuous ocean unfit for any water craft but the largest liners, yet to us it was a safe haven at last—the safest since we had left Fallon, Kansas, nine months and two days before.

It was our highway to the south and a livable world.

CHAPTER TWENTY-SEVEN

OUR COMPANY OF 37 survivors of the Fifth Ice Age sailed from Norfolk Complex on December 19th, 2204, and arrived at Lomita Complex, R.S.A. on December 31st, the last day of the year. But there were only thirty-six of us who saw the winds diminish and the snow turn to rain and who fell to our knees to offer our thanks to God when we first sighted the gray-green coast of the Province of Brazil.

The guiding spirit of our group, the one who had been wholly responsible for its formation and for the entire concept of our escape, as well as the escape of thousands of others, died on Christmas Day.

Gabe Harrow suffered a sudden relapse on the night of our departure from Norfolk Complex and it was Rufe Howard's opinion that it was brought on by his great exertions out in the storm to free us from the ice on those last terrible miles.

It was Gabe's last exertion and it was typical of his life that it was performed to help others. It was typical that he disregarded his own health and well being to perform a service for the common good.

It was ironical, too, that Gabe, one of the few who foresaw the awful storms and attempted to warn the world of the approaching disaster, was also one of the victims of his prophecy. He alone of the millions in his own community made the effort to save his life. He came close—only a few hundred miles from his goal at the Equator.

We buried Gabe Harrow at sea on Christmas night, we who were his last friends. And we cried unashamedly—Jack Osborne, Bob and Libby Jordan, Bill and Martha and Tony Wernecke, Marge, Perry and Sylvia Lawrence, Florence Donner, Rufe Howard and I—as his body slid quickly under the waves.

Once again I read the Order for the Burial of the Dead. It was not a good reading and I doubt that any heard my words as they were whipped from my mouth by the wind—a mere 55 miles per hour in that latitude.

Marge and I returned quickly to our cabin under the bridge and later Rufe Howard and Jack Osborne and Florence Donner joined us. We five sat and talked most of the rest of the night, trying to make plans for our life at the Equator. But they weren't inspired plans and our hearts weren't in them. Without Gabe Harrow we felt lost, without direction and without incentive.

There is not much else that can be said about our voyage South on the *Maecenas*. The ship behaved excellently in the furious seas of the North and logged a steady 250 miles per day with a minimum of pounding. But it was rough—don't let me mislead you on that point. These were no seas for a 175-foot yacht. Most of our company was seasick for the entire voyage despite the various drugs administered by Rufe Howard. The rest of us ran the ship and took care of the sick—and buried Gabe Harrow.

On December 31st we thirty-six disembarked at a new concrete pier at Lomita, which had replaced one destroyed the year before by the hurricane winds and ice. We stood around in a small group under a temporary shed out of the rain, and we looked shoreward to trees and earth—to things that grew and had life. I don't think that any of us had really believed he would ever see growing things again in this world.

That is my report of the Savage Company, from its inception as the Harrow Group down to its disbanding upon the pier at Lomita—from Fallon, Kansas to the Equator. Of our original party of twenty-three only twelve survived, and that is not a very good casualty record for any commander, no matter what the conditions. It is a record that I am not at all proud of, nor do I desire to mention the additional twenty-four from Kentucky Complex whom we helped save themselves, for then I am reminded of the twenty-eight whom we didn't bring with us to the R.S.A., and that is even a worse record of casualties.

It is well and good to excuse oneself on the grounds of the statistics—the thousands of millions who died all over Earth, but Gabe Harrow and Elaine and Alice Wernecke and the three Lawrences—Fred, Sam Houston and Georgia—and all the rest were not statistics. They were people I knew; they were friends—yes, even crazed Ali whom I executed in the East Barn with a converter.

So in a very important way to me it was no victory, and there was no cause for rejoicing except the very selfish one of having saved my own life and Marge's and the lives of our few friends remaining.

We have learned to live without the sun and we have become inured now to the wind and the rain and this foreign land. Life is not as sweet, perhaps, but the reason for that would lie within ourselves rather than with our environment, for our hosts have spared no effort to make us welcome.

Our fellow survivors from the North and the South have been given a home and all of the affection that goes with it. Perhaps some day we will learn to appreciate it adequately.

And perhaps some day our generations of the future will return to the North—when the snow stops and the ice recedes—and establish themselves again in the land that we once loved.

I hope they find it no less satisfying than we did.

THE END

If you've enjoyed this book, you will not want to miss these terrific titles…

ARMCHAIR SCI-FI & HORROR DOUBLE NOVELS, $12.95 each

D-31 **A HOAX IN TIME** by Keith Laumer
INSIDE EARTH by Poul Anderson

D-32 **TERROR STATION** by Dwight V. Swain
THE WEAPON FROM ETERNITY by Dwight V. Swain

D-33 **THE SHIP FROM INFINITY** by Edmond Hamilton
TAKEOFF by C. M. Kornbluth

D-34 **THE METAL DOOM** by David H. Keller
TWELVE TIMES ZERO by Howard Browne

D-35 **HUNTERS OUT OF SPACE** by Joseph Kelleam
INVASION FROM THE DEEP by Paul W. Fairman,

D-36 **THE BEES OF DEATH** by Robert Moore Williams
A PLAGUE OF PYTHONS by Frederick Pohl

D-37 **THE LORDS OF QUARMALL** by Fritz Leiber and Harry Fischer
BEACON TO ELSEWHERE by James H. Schmitz

D-38 **BEYOND PLUTO** by John S. Campbell
ARTERY OF FIRE by Thomas N. Scortia

D-39 **SPECIAL DELIVERY** by Kris Neville
NO TIME FOR TOFFEE by Charles F. Meyers

D-40 **RECALLED TO LIFE** by Robert Silverberg
JUNGLE IN THE SKY by Milton Lesser

ARMCHAIR SCIENCE FICTION CLASSICS, $12.95 each

C-10 **MARS IS MY DESTINATION**
by Frank Belknap Long

C-11 **SPACE PLAGUE**
by George O. Smith

C-12 **SO SHALL YE REAP**
by Rog Phillips

ARMCHAIR SCIENCE FICTION & HORROR GEMS SERIES, $12.95 each

G-3 **SCIENCE FICTION GEMS, Vol. Two**
James Blish and others

G-4 **HORROR GEMS, Vol. Two**
Joseph Payne Brennan and others

If you've enjoyed this book, you will not want to miss these terrific titles…

ARMCHAIR SCI-FI & HORROR DOUBLE NOVELS, $12.95 each

D-41   **FULL CYCLE** by Clifford D. Simak
        IT WAS THE DAY OF THE ROBOT by Frank Belknap Long

D-42   **THIS CROWDED EARTH** by Robert Bloch
        REIGN OF THE TELEPUPPETS by Daniel Galouye

D-43   **THE CRISPIN AFFAIR** by Jack Sharkey
        THE RED HELL OF JUPITER by Paul Ernst

D-44   **WE THE MACHINE** by Gerald Vance
        PLANET OF DREAD by Dwight V. Swain

D-45   **THE STAR HUNTER** by Edmond Hamilton
        THE ALIEN by Raymond F. Jones

D-46   **WORLD OF IF** by Rog Phillips
        SLAVE RAIDERS FROM MERCURY by Don Wilcox

D-47   **THE ULTIMATE PERIL** by Robert Abernathy
        PLANET OF SHAME by Bruce Elliot

D-48   **THE FLYING EYES** by J. Hunter Holly
        SOME FABULOUS YONDER by Phillip Jose Farmer

D-49   **THE COSMIC BUNGLERS** by Geoff St. Reynard
        THE BUTTONED SKY by Geoff St. Reynard

D-50   **TYRANTS OF TIME** by Milton Lesser
        PARIAH PLANET by Murray Leinster

ARMCHAIR SCIENCE FICTION CLASSICS, $12.95 each

C-13   **SUNKEN WORLD**
        by Stanton A. Coblentz

C-14   **THE LAST VIAL**
        by Sam McClatchie, M. D.

C-15   **WE WHO SURVIVED (THE FIFTH ICE AGE)**
        by Sterling Noel

ARMCHAIR MASTERS OF SCIENCE FICTION SERIES, $16.95 each

MS-5   **MASTERS OF SCIENCE FICTION, Vol. Five**
        Winston K. Marks—Test Colony and other tales

MS-6   **MASTERS OF SCIENCE FICTION, Vol. Six**
        Fritz Leiber—Deadly Moon and other tales